EASY TARGET

Laura took the deep sighing breath of exercise and turned to run down the knoll. Suddenly a pop of noise made a sharp sensation shoot across her upper arm. She grabbed her triceps and looked to the boulevard cliff, where the sound had come from. Around her feet the ground exploded with stinging gravel.

Someone on the cliff was shooting at her.

She dropped to the ground and scuttled backward to the safe side of the outcropping. Again she heard the popping of a gun.

Holding her upper arm, Laura lay on her back calling to the sky. "Mr. Talbot! Mr. Talbot!" Lots of help he was. She yelled again, then the horror crossed her mind: What if Detective Talbot was the one shooting at her . . . ?

BODY ENGLISH

LINDA MARIZ

CRIME LINE ™

BANTAM BOOKS

NEW YORK · TORONTO · LONDON · SYDNEY · AUCKLAND

BODY ENGLISH
A Bantam Crime Line Book / March 1992

ISBN 0-553-29700-7

Published simultaneously in the United States and Canada

PRINTED IN THE UNITED STATES OF AMERICA

RAD 0 9 8 7 6 5 4 3 2 1

To George

CHAPTER 1

The bimbos were everywhere. A morning sweep of the mens' locker room found one who had slept there. Three in short shorts buzzed the university dock in a speedboat. Tom Selleck was coming to volleyball Nationals; nobody knew whether to be excited or disgusted.

The two women on the Seattle field house steps had no use for bimbos. Their names were Terri and Bushman and they cared only about volleyball. They could win Nationals this year—if spiker Laura Ireland showed up. If she didn't, they'd have to make do with Terri's little sister, a stretched-out seventeen-year-old named Rookie.

"God, she's a flake." Terri was pissed at Laura.

"She's coming," said Bushman. "She just couldn't leave L.A. until this morning. They have her teaching freshman anthro."

"Anthro, swell. And when she does get here, are you going to tell her about her dead professor?"

"Not right away," said Bushman. "Let's get a few good games out of her first."

Terri looked at her watch. It was forty minutes until opening match, already teams were warming up on the floor. Reaching back for her French braid, she put the tip in her mouth. Bushman was right, no telling how Laura would react about the dead professor, better to keep quiet for a while. Terri threw back the tip of her braid and began gnawing her fingernails.

Bushman said, "Terri, think about something else. Have you heard of the team we're playing?"

"Malibu Beach Associates. Somebody said they're good."

"*We're* good."

"Bushman, we haven't played serious ball for four years now."

"Doesn't matter. When I was counting bodies to see who's here, I realized Laura is sixth best spiker in the country. And I might be about fourth best in middle court."

"Who're you counting ahead of you, the national team?"

"And they're touring Asia."

"Leaving the tournament open for us has-beens."

"Think about something else."

A cab pulled up and after a glance at the backseat passenger, Bushman and Terri looked away. A blonde in a creamy suit, hair out to there, paid the driver and started up the stairs in their direction. Because they were embarrassed for her—dressing like that for a volleyball tournament—Bushman and Terri looked away, far across the parking lots. The blonde kept coming and stopped in front of them on the steps below.

"Bushman? Terri?" she said. "It's me, Laura."

No one spoke. Laura's hair was a blonde Hollywood mane teased up and out and down her back. The makeup was smooth and professional, her cheekbones sculpted in soft blush. She smiled a tinted apricot smile and blinked her blackened lashes.

"Jesus, woman, what have you done to yourself?"

"I just got off an airplane. I thought I looked pretty good."

"Good for what? My Lord, we gotta get you out of that. Come on, you're late." Bushman grabbed Laura's garment bag and tramped off through the crowded foyer.

If anyone could clear a path for them it was Bushman. Broad-shouldered and six-three, she was good at intimidating the opposition. With pale skin and blue-black hair, Bushman cultivated her natural ferocity even further by perming her hair into an Afro and letting her eyebrows grow together into a black smear across her forehead. All this, coupled with a nervous habit of twitching her wrists when she was cross or upset, usually got Bushman whatever she wanted.

In contrast to Bushman the competent giant, Terri was a classic setter. Acutely responsive to the people around her, both on and off the court, what set Terri apart was her egg-shell fineness, her apparent fragility marked by blue-stained hollows under her eyes. Back when she played international ball, coaches used the darkness of these hollows as indicators of the whole team's fatigue.

Laura, golden Laura, they both adored. Six-feet-one, with limbs long enough to kill, Laura was kidded mercilessly about her slate-blue eyes, chiseled cheekbones, and head of yellow hair. When the three of them used to tour with the national team, photographers always focused on Laura and little girls asked for her autograph. The famous photograph of an airborne Laura riveting her killshot into three Romanian blockers graced desk tops as far away as Washington, D.C. No one resented the attention to Laura, especially since Laura herself thought it so ridiculous. Men avoided her, as they avoided all tall women, and she was so insecure about her flat chest and boyish hips it didn't make any sense to begrudge Laura her pretty face.

Bushman wormed and wove through the crowd until she was stopped by a beefy security guard at the top of the basement stairs. There she waited for the other two so that she and Terri could vouch for Laura. There was no way the guard wouldn't think Laura, dressed as she was, was hot for a bit part in *Magnum, P.I.*

"She's with us," said Bushman.

The guard eyed Laura skeptically but grunted for them to pass. Laura was surprised. "What's the security for? It's like playing in Korea."

"Didn't you hear? Tom Selleck's coming to play with the Outrigger Canoe Club in Honolulu."

"Tom Selleck? Oh God, I haven't thought about him in ages. Is he still wearing love handles on his tummy?"

"Cut it out, Laura, you know you salivate every time you see him. Do you still have his poster in your locker?"

"I only bought it because he donated the proceeds to the national team."

"Yeah, and you only got it autographed to see if your pen was working."

Terri listened to the two friends rag each other as they breezed into the dressing room and began banging open locker doors. Back in their national team days Laura and Bushman had been roommates, Laura being the one who had named Bushman the day she returned from the beauty parlor with her amazing hairdo.

As Terri scanned locker tops for a hanger for Laura's jacket, she wondered what kind of life Laura led in Los Angeles now that she wore cream-colored silk on airplanes. But life was now different for all of them. She herself had some big news to tell, but not yet; it wasn't time. Bush and Laura were still talking Tom Selleck, Bushman totally ignoring the dead anthropology professor that Laura used to like, or maybe still liked. Terri found a place to break in.

"You guys are being too critical. I don't think Selleck had anything a couple of hundred sit-ups couldn't fix."

"Couple of thousand," said Laura.

"He probably has it off by now," said Terri.

Bushman didn't care much for men's bodies, so she took the role of group conscience. "Listen, I refuse to stand here and talk about this guy's abs when we don't really know him. We sound like the bimbos."

"Agreed," said Terri, and she and Bushman watched from the corner of their eyes as Laura peeled off the ivory silk skirt and Charmeuse blouse. Then came off the lacy ecru slip, creamy kidskin heels, and ivory panty hose. By the time she was down to her cotton panties and flat little girl's chest, they knew they had their Laura back, Laura the volleyball player, sixth best spiker in the country. Terri threw Laura a pair of black bunhuggers and a powder blue jersey.

Laura held up the jersey and read, " 'Gatoraders, Gainesville, Florida.' Well, thank you, Gatorade; just remember to send the check before my Visa bill arrives."

She sat down to tie her Nikes while Terri took a hairbrush to the Hollywood do. Except for Bushman, they all wore single French braids when playing: A braid bounced less than a ponytail and—if started high enough on the head—even cushioned a little on floor rolls.

"I can do that," said Laura.

"Be quiet, we're in a hurry."

Terri plaited in silence, bound the blonde rope, then hurried Laura off to the playing floor of the University of Washington's Hec Edmondson field house. The huge floor was set up with six volleyball nets and surrounded by a balcony of nine thousand folding seats. Laura looked from end to end, then up to the rafters where soundproof padding and a digital scoreboard were the only touch of modernity.

"Place is old," said Laura.

"At least the floor's level," said Bush. And they all snickered, thinking of the gyms in Poland.

Bushman picked up a ball and passed it to Laura. Laura bumped back without thinking. "Who we playing?"

"They're called Malibu Associates but I can't get a fix on them at all. Too old to be a college team. When I went over to eavesdrop all they talked about was missing the soap operas today. Look, there they are."

Malibu wore lemon-colored jerseys, same color as the Clairol on their hair. They were tall enough to be volleyball players but—unlike most players—were leathery and broad, missing some sort of legged elegance. Cigarette stink wafted from those who came over to shag balls.

"They look more like a basketball team," said Laura.

"I was thinking motorcycle gang myself."

"Bushman, what if they're good?"

"They do seem pro, don't they? Look, that one won't even jump unless she has to."

The trio of Gatoraders grew sober at the thought that there

might be competition at a tournament they planned to walk away with. They bumped light passes back and forth while the rest of the Gainesville Gatoraders—two Karens, a Lisa, and a Kim—took their first look at this Laura they'd heard so much about from Terri, their assistant coach at the University of Florida.

Laura knew the college girls were watching and tried to pass with the same motion each time so they could get used to her moves. Then she noticed Terri's parents, the Watts, up in the stands. She waved and Mrs. Watt waved cheerfully back. The Watts were retired Floridians who followed their girls' athletics everywhere—except to Romania where they hadn't been allowed. This is like old times, thought Laura. But there was someone else sitting with the Watts. "Terri, who's that guy with your parents?"

"He's Norman, our chiropractor. Gatorade paid his way."

"Terri!"

"No, really. It's for our backs. I told Gatorade some of us were in our late twenties and might have trouble. Chiropractors give great massages."

Bushman wasn't going to let it pass. "Terri, tell her the real news."

Terri reddened and looked at the floor. "Norman and I are going to be married."

"When? Oh God, I'm squealing, when?"

"We haven't set a date yet."

"That's great." Laura grinned up at Norman and waved. Norman pushed his glasses up his nose and waved back.

They watched Malibu walk through blocking practice, barely raising their skinny arms or leaving the floor. It was unsettling to see effort conserved like that when Malibu should be warming up. These were athletes, no doubt about it, but not quite volleyball players. Laura was reminded of a herd of giraffes, listless and yellow and slow-moving.

"Bushman, look how everyone on Malibu is alike."

"I saw that. But look around the gym, all the teams are like that. See that purple team? All short Asian girls with 'power' thighs."

"Guess they've been hitting the Nautilus machines.

'Rainbow Wahines,' '' Laura read. "It's the University of Hawaii.''

Laura looked at her uniform and the huddle of tall Floridians dressed like her. "I wonder if we all look alike.''

"You guys do, for sure. Every one of you is blonde, white bread, wears a French braid.''

"I'm not white bread.''

"God, Laura, Wonderbread got the idea from looking at you.''

They moved on to tossing digs to each other, Laura happy and humming. Nobody in Los Angeles ribbed her like that. In graduate school everyone was too busy to kid, not like athletes at all. Bumping the ball again with Bush gave her the overwhelming desire to drop the Ph.D. program and spend the rest of her life on a volleyball court.

Terri came over for setting practice and worked Laura quickly through as many angles as they both could think of. "You remember my sister, Rookie?" asked Terri. "She's gonna sub for us.''

"She a setter too?''

"Since fourth grade, but she says she's sick of it. She only came here because I said she could spike. She made high school all-American this spring.''

"She excited?''

"Rookie doesn't get excited about anything, thinks all that stuff is her birthright. Back when I made all-American they gave us jackets—watch my feet—and when they didn't give them out this year Rookie wanted to write and complain. Momma wouldn't let her.''

The buzzer sounded for lineup and Laura found a place between the sisters. The last time Laura had seen Rookie she was five-feet-two.

"Hi, Rookie, remember me?''

"Sure.''

"How tall are you now?''

"Five-ten.''

"Finished?''

"Yeah.''

"Too bad.''

The referee glared, so Rookie whispered. "I got a scholarship to Florida State."

"Way to go, babe."

The ref began the proceedings, indicating first serve to Malibu, side choice to Gatoraders.

Terri was coaching since this was her gig and, without consciously thinking, jotted down a 5–1 lineup—five hitters and a setter—that gave the Gatoraders the second strongest rotation in volleyball—Laura spiking out of left front, herself setting at right back and ever-hustling Bushman middle-blocking out of center back. The rest of the slots she filled in with her college team, Karen and Karen-Two in the front line and Kimmy in left backcourt. Rookie and Lisa sat on the bench.

On the first serve Malibu sent over a floater between Kimmy and Bushman near the center seam. Bushman stepped aside to let Kimmy pick it out. Kimmy turned expectantly to Bushman and stood watching as it dropped to the floor: She had fully expected Bushman and Laura to handle everything round and white that flew. The Gatoraders exchanged surprised looks and realized they had to play volleyball together.

"S'okay. Teamwork." And they hand-slapped high and low and got into "ready" again.

The next serve came down the line where Bushman stepped back to pass it crisply up to Terri. To be extra sure they got it right this time, Terri called out.

"Laura."

They all knew what was coming next.

Out in the sidelines Laura started her quick approach with a short step for momentum, a long one for velocity, all the while from the corner of her eye watching the leaping and swinging Bushman faking through the air above center court. The Malibu block began congealing across from Laura.

Taking off three feet from the net, Laura leapt forward to meet Terri's set. Telegraphing midcourt with her eyes, she aimed a killing spike off the elbow of the outside blocker.

At the last second the outside Malibu blocker put her hand out to break up Laura's shot. The ball bounced back onto Laura's head and dribbled down her backside.

Kimmy, behind her, stumbled up the floor and dug the

ball out inches from the brown linoleum. She bumped it to Terri at the net who readied herself for a jump set, then shunted it quickly over herself. En masse, Malibu splatted to the midcourt floor but still missed the hit. Terri cursed at having to give away a good move so early.

The Gatoraders looked at each other in surprise. The Malibu block was hard and high, as good as an international team. What's more, Malibu knew who Laura was, they had been watching the videos. This was going to be tougher than they thought. Laura glanced the question at Bushman: *Who are these people?*

Bushman shrugged.

The referee left the court to recover the ball because no one from Malibu would go. Laura tested the net with her long fingers and spoke to the player on the other side.

"Y'guys are good, you tour or something?"

"No way. We all used to do skateboard in junior high together, now we all live on the beach."

"Far out."

Laura bent over and touched her toes to think. No wonder these women blocked like a stone wall: They knew each other like mirror images and they jumped on sand every day of the year. Terri came over and said, "Let's move the set around, see if they can follow."

Laura grinned. "Waltz time."

"And see if you can hesitate some tips to backcourt. If they play on the beach, they don't want to bounce off this floor too much."

"I don't want to bounce off this floor either."

"Hard, isn't it?"

The game started up again, this time with a roaming team of Gatoraders setting from odd-tempo tips all the way across the forecourt. The strategy confused Malibu's block enough for the Gatoraders to rack up points, gaining four to Malibu's one, then seven to Malibu's four. Malibu read the new offense and starting calling out noisy shifts. They worked with fitful success and when the score reached Gatoraders 11, Malibu 5, Malibu called time-out.

On the next volley Malibu's tallest blocker left her post to bird-dog Laura. All other Malibu players had chosen quarry too. Terri and Laura exchanged swift grins and both turned to Bushman. On the next ball Bushman pulled back for a quick approach and Terri set up to an empty slot at midnet. Appearing out of nowhere, Bushman smashed the ball into the arms of her single Malibu blocker. The confused Malibu players buzzed in a huddle. Bushman turned around so they wouldn't see her smile.

The younger Gatoraders knew some turning point had come but couldn't tell exactly what it was. They huddled around Terri, who explained: "We broke their defense. They expected their three-man block to work all day long. Now they see man-to-man won't work either."

The Gatoraders took three straight points, making the score 14–5, then lost their concentration. Taking over the serve, Malibu pushed back to 14–8. Finally, after a long aimless volley, Bushman rallied, putting the ball away with a vicious backcourt slash that galvanized the rest of the Gatoraders. They took back the serve and, after a brief volley, the game.

Afterward Laura sat slumped in a chair squirting water into her mouth. She had forgotten how hard volleyball was, how much concentration was needed for every single point. It was as hard as a dissertation.

Bushman sat down too and squirted water on her face. "You look good, Ireland, you been working out with UCLA?"

"You mean the women? No, I watched them once, they're weenies. I found some nice tall guys in the gym, though."

"You dating anybody down there?"

"Right. And when have you ever cared?"

"No reason. Say, I forgot to tell you: If we win two out of three this afternoon we have a 'bye' and are free all day tomorrow. I called my mother and told her I'd be coming up to Bellingham. Want to go with me, visit your old stomping grounds?"

Laura hid her alarm. Bushman's father was the anthropology chairman at Western University, where Laura had done her master's degree. Did Bushman know the trouble she was having now with Professor Larry Todd, her old mentor in that department?

"Nice offer, Bush, but no thanks. I'll read or something."

By the middle of the second game, Malibu knew they were beat. Whenever the defense prepared their wall for Laura or Bushman, the tip would rise up in a neat little arc and roll down their backsides to the floor. When Malibu backcourt moved up to cover the tip, Bushman and Laura, and then increasingly the college girls, aimed for the deserted backcourts and three times out of four found an undefended spot to lay the ball in. It was classic volleyball, clean and simple, with just enough finesse for the younger players to learn on. At 9–3 Terri took out Bushman and Laura and substituted Lisa and Rookie. Rookie was so hyper she high-fived everybody, waved at her parents, and touched her shoe tips twice.

On the sidelines Bushman and Laura sat with towels on their heads to hurry sweat along. "Glad to get off the floor," said Laura. "That baby's hard on the knees."

Bushman pressed the brown linoleum with her fingertips. "No wonder: It's laid over concrete." Then she looked at Laura to see how she'd take the next bit of news. "Got something to tell you. I knew it would rattle you, so I didn't mention it before, but guess what else Mom said this morning on the phone?"

"Hmm?"

"Larry Todd is dead. He got shot over the weekend and the funeral was this morning."

CHAPTER 2

Laura spoke through a cardboard smile. "Bushman, I can't believe you'd do this, it's so embarrassing."

"Just lift the sign. You're doing great."

From the parking garage in front of them a gray Toyota pulled into the daylight. The driver was a plump fortyish woman squinting in the sunshine.

"Smile, Laura, this is the one we want." Bushman had no idea why Laura had changed her mind about hitchhiking to Bellingham this Tuesday afternoon, but having her along certainly did make it easier. Laura bared her teeth and held the Bellingham sign to her chest.

The driver stopped beside them and rolled down the window. Bushman and Laura found themselves staring down the cleft of a huge ivory bosom. The driver said, "I'm going there, to Bellingham, but I will be practicing the cassette tapes on the way home." She had an odd Germanic accent and listened to her own voice as she spoke. Picking at the lavender ruffles around her cleavage, she said, "My music lessons are on the cassettes. It will be all right with you?"

Bushman hustled Laura into the backseat. "No problem. We like music. We'll sit back here so we don't bother you."

The two tall women stuffed in their bags, found places for their legs, then sat quietly as the German lady pulled into four o'clock traffic. They watched as she punched in a cassette of piano arpeggios and then—after listening a minute—try to stretch her larynx around the trills.

At first Bushman and Laura were overwhelmed with the singing: the astounding bosom swelling up with air, and shrinking down with sound. When trill practice was over they looked on mutely as the soprano took out the first tape and inserted another, this time trying to mimic a baritone light-years better than she. But when Marta—that was her name—put in the third tape to practice an aria, measure by painful measure, they stopped listening and realized they could talk in low voices without offending her.

"So how's UCLA?" said Bushman.

"UCLA is exactly what it says it is, a great big education factory."

"Don't you like it?"

"It's fine. But I'd certainly like to stop breathing Los Angeles."

"Dad asks about you whenever I see him. I think his department uses you as an example of the kind of master's student they like to produce."

"Actually there's some exciting news for him. When I met the photo archivist at the East-West Center in Honolulu and told him my dissertation topic, he said we might talk about collaborating on a book when I finish."

"Tell me your topic again."

"Bilateralism in Pacific Rim Art with Reference to the Shang Dynasty."

"Cute."

"Anyway. The archivist showed me a book he and Delbert Shane did on Polynesian religions and it was gorgeous. He thinks bilateralism is a good topic for photo treatment—he'd do photos, I'd do text—and if he can make bilateralism look as good as religions, I'd really be excited. So tell your father at this point things look pretty good.''

"That's good to hear, but maybe *you'd* better tell my father.'' Bushman paused for emphasis. "We don't speak too much anymore.''

"Bush, what's wrong?''

"Mom moved into her apartment. I think they're really going to do it this time.''

"That's too bad. How's your mom taking it?''

"Not very well. She still lets him walk all over her and every time I come home there's some new crisis: He wants his mother's china, or the reading lamp, or some recipe he can use to impress his girlfriend. Mom's so out of it she just stays in bed and cries, doesn't even buy groceries and stuff.''

"Wait a minute, if she's got an apartment, does she have room for both of us?''

"No problem, the couch makes into a double bed. Mom'll be happy to see you.''

Laura bit her lip. She had spent most of her volleyball career sharing too-small beds with other too-tall women and had vowed never to do it again. To hide her guilty thoughts she said, "Well, maybe now your mom will do something with her art.''

"I hope so,'' said Bushman. "When I was little I used to watch her sketch and always wished I were more like her and less like him.'' Bushman looked at her steely forearms and big square knees. Most of what made her so formidable and athletic came from her tall, black-haired father.

They listened to Marta again and in a minute Bushman sensed it was Laura's turn to tell. But Laura stared blindly out the window.

Bushman made an attempt, "You really liked Larry Todd, didn't you?''

Laura answered cautiously. "He was my thesis adviser and I couldn't have changed from physical education without him. He really gave me a lot of his time.'' Again she looked away so Bushman couldn't see how she was paying for that time.

"That's not what I meant. You're not coming to Bellingham today to be near where he died, are you?''

"Bush, if you don't mind, I don't want to talk about it. I really have mixed feelings." So mixed, in fact, she remembered one day—the worst day of her life—when she wrote him first a love letter, then a letter threatening to kill him. She remembered hating Todd, hating herself so much, she raged around with a chef's knife, jabbing holes in her brand-new king-size mattress.

Bushman tried lightheartedness: "I bet you liked Larry Todd because he was so tall. You really get snowed by guys bigger than us."

"Larry was much more than just a tall person. I had—still have—a great deal of respect for him."

"You, and everybody else. The way my dad talks, you'd think Larry was Mr. Anthropology, being so famous and going to all those conferences and stuff. And languages: Dad goes crazy when people do languages."

"Larry was very talented, people were drawn to him. And maybe if I hadn't been such an ignorant gym puppy when I met him I could have made a better companion for him."

"Really? I thought he was kind of a con artist myself."

"Larry was a very complicated person. You didn't know him like I did."

"You're forgetting I've known him since I was sixteen."

The conversation ended in a standoff. In a minute Bushman turned again to Laura and said, "You still haven't told me why you changed you mind about coming to Bellingham."

"To visit."

"Ha."

"To see the anthropology department."

"Ha. I bet you're in trouble or something."

"No."

"You lie. I can tell by your voice."

Laura measured Bushman's face for trust. "Actually I am a little bit."

"What'd you do?"

Laura glanced at Marta huffing in the front seat. To be extra sure they weren't overhead she slumped down, motioning for Bushman to follow. "Bushman, I'm in the worst trouble since that time with the airport guards in Bucharest. I'm walking in it so deep I'm up to my eustachian tubes.''

''Fallopian tubes.''

''You heard me.''

''What happened?''

She opened her mouth to tell Bushman about the letters she had written when suddenly Marta spoke. ''The gasoline says 'Empty.' I will be stopping at the Texaco down there.''

Laura and Bushman sat up to get their bearings. They were in Mount Vernon, thirty miles south of Bellingham. Marta steered into the station and Bushman started to get out. ''We can pump for you.''

''No,'' said Marta, ''I am at the full-service island. Men like it better if you sit in the car.'' She checked her ruffles.

The attendant came over and Marta lowered her window. Bush and Laura watched the man's eyes dilate. ''Yes, ma'am?''

''Fill it up, please,'' said Marta. ''The tank is on the other side by that young lady back there.''

''Yes, ma'am.'' The attendant glanced back at Laura, who looked away.

Marta excused herself and Bushman and Laura were left alone with the attendant who pumped gas a pane of glass away.

''So tell me what you did,'' demanded Bushman.

''Well, I wrote love letters to Larry Todd.''

''Who cares?''

''In the letters I talked about his Indian artifacts business.''

''And?''

''Selling artifacts isn't exactly professional for an anthropologist.''

Bushman shrugged.

Laura looked away to the yellow gorgeousness of the Skagit Valley flower fields. If Bushman could have helped her out of the mess she was in over Larry's artifact business she would have told her the truth. For the truth was that Todd had involved her in his illegal business and she'd been dumb enough to help.

Three years ago, when she had first asked him about the

duffel bag of rattles, masks, and blankets he stowed in the hatch of his Boston Whaler, he told her it was just a little something he did to help the Indians. Then, under further pressure, as she watched him work magic on Kwakiutl alcoholics with his green American twenties, he told her how he helped certain Indian families by giving them cash for their unwanted objects. There was very little currency in the economy, he said, it was the outsider's job to supply it.

But, she had asked, wouldn't this encourage the removal of the most important objects from a culture? Oh no, he assured her. For the most part the Indians were playing a huge game with white buyers. The Kwakiutls would turn out freshly carved masks, rattles, whatever, rub tobacco juice on them and present them as highly prized antique artifacts. Wasn't that a good joke on whitey?

Yes, she supposed, it was a good joke, and she had sat quietly in the boat, watching Larry unzip the canvas duffel, taking out the green twenties and putting back the best the Kwakiutls had to offer.

Then, a few months later he had asked her to help him with some errands. Could she take some crates through customs for him and handle the paperwork? Certainly, she'd be glad to. After all, they were sleeping together by then and he had taken her intellectual life firmly in hand, moving her at a breathtaking clip through the history of anthropological theory, all the while insisting that she learn to express herself on paper in clearheaded academic prose.

Three times she shuffled crates through customs for him, only to happy to help the overburdened Larry with his work. But by the third trip, as she stood in the customs office actually reading the declarations, she realized Larry was doing something that required outright lying: Instead of listing the artifacts that Laura knew to be in the crates, he had represented the contents as digging supplies, reference books, and camping equipment. Suddenly numb with understanding—not only about the artifact business, but also about their relationship—Laura watched herself stonily sign for the shipment and send it on its way.

After that things went downhill fast. Laura tearfully confronted Larry about the crates and then about the wife he still hadn't divorced. He was apologetic at first, then annoyed, finally downright vicious. He cut her off swiftly, saying she would regret ever turning on him.

The gasoline attendant started cussing. "Jesus Christ, what'n the—" Gasoline poured down onto the concrete.

Bushman snorted. "Serves him right, he's been staring at you the whole time, Laura."

Laura shrugged. Long ago she learned to pretend she didn't understand what was happening in such situations. Watching the attendant mop the fender with a rag, she silently compared his five-eight frame to Larry's tall one: *That's okay, fellow, you don't know how fast you'd run if I stood up beside you.*

Marta came back and maneuvered the car onto the highway. In a few minutes Bushman tried once more. "Had you been keeping up with Larry, for old time's sake?"

In the front seat Marta stretched her upper lip and exhaled Italian onto the mirror. *"Prendi, per me sei libero. Pren-di, pren-di."* She was having problems saying *"prendi."*

Laura answered carefully. "He'd call occasionally, just to keep up with my work." Her work—right: Two weeks ago Todd had called for the first time ever and asked her to receive a shipment of crates for him. She was so furious she screamed into the phone and hung up.

Five minutes later he had called back with an entirely new tone, serious and sinister, calling her "sister," as in "Listen, sister, I have in my hands sweet letters from one Ms. Laura Ireland which indicate she, of her own free will, misrepresented customs shipments and even took artifacts from the Keena dig." Through the phone she could hear his duffel unzipping: "Here we are." His voice became stagy and sarcastic as he read: " 'Dear Larry, I know now it was wrong to take the bracelets across the line without telling the Georges.' "

"Larry, you asked me to take those bracelets."

"Not that I can see. Nope, according to these letters, you did it all by yourself. Here's one, 'Tuesday, April third, I'm sorry I talked Jimmy B. into carving those fish clubs. Smuggling crates like that makes me ashamed to be white.' Oh, is the poor girl ashamed? Well, listen, sisterbelle, I don't know what profession you thought you were going to join, but when our anthropology chums see how you manipulate your subject culture, they won't be letting you anywhere near the A's. Or maybe I'll send this shit down to your UCLA adviser with a little note—Timberlake, isn't it? I can explain that you had financial troubles and really hadn't meant to steal . . .''

Laura's heart had beat so hard she couldn't talk. Once again she hung up on him, this time mute with pain.

For two weeks she had lived in constant dread, waiting for the phone call, the penciled note from Dr. Timberlake. Could Larry really do that? It was just his word against hers. But he had written proof—and he was a real anthropologist. She had sat in front of the word processor, staring at the blipping cursor, not writing a word of her dissertation.

But the days passed and nothing came of Larry's threat. After a brief respite, she realized yet another numbing thought: For her whole professional life Larry Todd had a threat to use against her whenever he chose. What's more, the better established she became in the profession, the further Larry's letters would cause her to fall. How long, she had reflected, would Larry Todd be a threat? Until, she realized, he was dead.

But now he *was* dead, and there was still a threat. In the single second on the sideline today when Bushman told her about his death, Laura saw what the new danger was: Someone would gain possession of Larry's books and papers, *and* her letters. That person would be Larry's hateful wife, Barbara—Barbara, who had known Laura was her rival even before she herself did. Laura took a deep breath.

Bushman said, "I get it."

"Get what?"

"You're going back to get your love letters, aren't you?"

"Bushman, what if I can't find them?"

"I'll help you. I know how to talk my way past Dad."

Laura bit her lip.

Marta had passed through the Chuckanut Hills which signaled the southern approach to Bellingham. She glanced into the rearview mirror to query her passengers, but before she could speak, Laura leaned forward.

"Marta, excuse me. Could you let me out at the mall?

I'm going to call a friend from there." She turned to Bushman. "I've been thinking: You and your mom need to be alone right now and I'd feel like an extra thumb staying with you. I'll stay with somebody from intramurals." Marta obligingly pulled up by a bank of phone booths and Laura got out.

Bushman was stunned. "Wait, Laura, I can help. And there's something else I want to tell you about my father."

Laura pulled out her garment bag, "That's okay, Bush, I know pretty much how the department runs. If I have time I'll call you later tonight; we can go to a movie or something."

CHAPTER 3

Ho Kauffmann was a short gay Jewish philologist, and one of the best friends Laura had ever had. As her downstairs neighbor and first acquaintance in Bellingham, Ho had helped her carry books and a king-size mattress up steep stairs to her third-floor apartment. And after that, for a very brief time, he had even curled up with her in sleeping there. But that was later, after Larry Todd had explained that he really hadn't meant to say he was divorcing his wife, only that he should.

Laura found a pay phone and punched Ho Kauffmann's number. It was answered after the first ring.

"Ho Kauffmann speaking."

"Laura Ireland speaking."

"Laura, where on earth are you? Are you all right?"

"I'm at the mall, can you come and get me? I need a place to stay for the night and I was hoping for your couch."

"Then you've come about Larry Todd. But you've missed the funeral, it was this morning."

"I know about all that, but that's not why I'm here. I'm playing volleyball in Seattle and managed to wangle a free day. I have to be back day after tomorrow."

"But this is so sudden. The apartment is a mess—"

"Ho, you know very well I don't care what your apartment looks like."

"Of course you don't, and you're entirely welcome to stay. I'll be right down."

Laura hung up and went to a bank of newspaper machines for a *Bellingham Tribune*. There weren't many outright murders in a town of forty thousand and Larry Todd's death was bound to make good reading until at least the end of the week. Scanning the front-page headlines, she found no mention of Todd's name. She searched the news section, then turned to "Friends and Neighbors" to see if he was at least gossip. But Larry Todd's name was nowhere to be found.

The May afternoon was turning to evening. Laura sniffed the cooling air and listened to the highway take on night noises. Humming tires echoed off the hills and downshifting eighteen-wheelers gave full notice of their labors on the grade. Shadows were deeper here, between the hills of town, and the automobiles—suddenly aware of the progress of the evening—switched on their headlights as they entered the valley. After a while Ho pulled up in his red Honda.

Laura ran to the passenger door and quickly slipped in.

"Laura dear, you look wonderful."

Laura flashed a pearly smile and leaned over to kiss the cheek of the birdlike little man. He kissed back, pressing his nose against her face.

"So good to see you, Ho, you haven't changed at all."

"Is that so? You've just gotten better-looking."

"Thank you, nice man."

"Bah."

Ho steered the car through the crowds arriving for the six o'clock movie. When he had the Honda out on the street and revved smoothly through the gears, he spoke again.

"It's flattering that you called, I know you have lots of friends in the anthro department."

"Ho Kauffmann, cut that out. You know very well when Larry dropped me the rest of them started treating me like a social disease."

"Nonsense. Every time I'm down there someone asks about you. They see you as their rising star, gone on to bigger and better things."

"Certainly bigger. I still can't get used to a campus that needs a daily newspaper."

"How big is UCLA now?"

"Thirty-three thousand, ten thousand of that graduate school."

"Hm, bet the library's good."

"Not as good as you might think, I had to go to Berkeley twice and Honolulu once."

"Berkeley, yes, it's awfully good in my field too. I've taken to summering in the Bay Area."

"Ho, for the life of me I never understood what your field is all about. What do you do besides getting to read anything you please?"

Half-closing his eyes with pleasures, Ho contemplated his favorite topic. "Basically we are in the business of judging the authenticity of texts. The problem is that each century for the past five has defined our task differently. In this century we haven't agreed to methodology yet, only concurring— rather smugly—that we do a better job than they did in the past. So, while we're waiting for our results to come in, let's just say that we are looking for a few good metaphors."

"Do you really just sit there waiting for metaphors to turn up? Seems like it would get a little boring."

"Oh, not boring, perhaps a little lonely though."

Laura glanced sideways to see his face. "I can imagine." Then she said, "Did you go to the funeral this morning?"

"That I elected to avoid."

"You didn't really know Larry very well, did you?"

He was silent a moment. "Actually," he said, "I've seen more of Todd since you've left than I ever would have thought. This last year he had associations with the fringe element of our crowd."

"Larry was *not* gay."

"No, he used our contacts for what he said was 'pharmacological research.' "

"I don't understand."

"He really wanted to buy drugs, dear."

"Really? He was so talented. He used to talk about doing cross-cultural drug research. He even had me organize all the peyote literature for him."

"Laura dear, you'll never know how much I used to worry about you when you were so closely under his tutelage. I often wondered if I should have said something about your choices."

"My choices were great. And I couldn't have done it without Larry."

"That may well be, but even at this late date when I try to describe my tall blonde athletic friend, I'm at a loss to explain why someone with your physical skills would choose to retrain in a field like anthropology. I wondered if Todd was some sort of Svengali-type figure . . ."

"Wait a minute, are you trying to say there's something wrong with anthropology?"

"Nothing a few hundred years of scholarship won't cure. My point is that anthropology is so far afield from athletics."

"You mean I never told you why I changed fields?"

"Never."

"I'm sure I must have told you how I got my eyes opened when we toured internationally."

"Oh, that."

"Ho, you don't understand how dumb I was. I mean, I can actually remember being proud of the fact that I knew six different ways to tie my shoelaces: We're talking dumb jock."

"You've only showed me two ways."

"I remember once on our Asian tour I watched a Japanese coach yell at a player and she bowed to him when he was finished. Right then, I realized I didn't know anything. I felt so vulnerable. And then I started noticing whole bunches of things like that: How American-style laughing can make you look like an oaf, why Asian women don't seem to mind the way they're treated. Anthropology forces you into a discipline of vulnerability; I like that."

"Well, I'm sure you're making wonderful inroads, and you've made an excellent decision in choosing UCLA."

Laura remembered the newspaper in the backseat. "Ho, I can't find anything about Larry in the *Tribune*. When Bushman said he died this weekend, I thought for sure he'd still be a hot item. It's only Tuesday."

"There's an article: front page, right side. But I did notice that today's the first day he's been below the fold."

Laura squinted, trying to visualize the *Tribune*'s first page. "Below the fold was an article about a missing woman."

"Yes, that's it, the woman whose trailer he was found in. She's the assumed killer and is still at large."

"Wow." Laura dug her hands into the pockets of her warm-ups. "Wonder what he did to her."

"Sounds like a ghastly situation, doesn't it? She's a barmaid or some such, and Todd was found lying on her bed with a rather picturesque shotgun hole in his middle. Very close range, they said, 'About an hour after dinner on Saturday.' Sounds like they autopsied his stomach, doesn't it? And yesterday the *Tribune* titillated us with the news that it's not really her bed, or even her trailer. It's her ex-husband's and she only lives there when he's working in Alaska. At this point the police can't even find him."

Ho turned into one of the narrow alleys running off the steep slope of South Hill. Halfway down the block he eased the car into a parking niche between dumpsters and a garden wall. From here in the alley—behind and above the street—Ho's second-floor apartment in the Victorian Endicott House was walk-in level.

Endicott House was one of the dozen or so Victorians that had escaped the wrecker's ball. Built by lumberman George Endicott with San Francisco earthquake profits, Endicott House was still owned and cared for by Endicott's granddaughter, Alida Morse, who lived in antique refinement in a first-floor apartment.

Laura pulled her garment bag out of the car before Ho could grab it. "Can we go down front, Ho? I'd love to see how the old girl is holding up."

"You mean the house and not the woman, I trust? You'll be pleased; they've done some wonderful things down there."

Ho and Laura picked their way down the lighted rockery steps and through the shadows of Mrs. Morse's rose garden. They came around to the front of the hulking mauve monstrosity to admire its gingerbread carpentry, three-story turret, and lighted art glass windows.

"Mrs. Morse got the porch redone! They did such a good job. Who's up on the third floor now?"

"A mathematician and his wife; she works in the library."

"Are they nice?" Laura tested the handrail.

"Not as nice as my old neighbor."

They entered the paneled foyer and wiped their feet on the worn Ardebil carpet at the foot of the stairs. Signs of Mrs. Morse were everywhere: tea rose potpourri scented the foyer and pink parrot tulips fought for air in a massive silver pot. When Laura had lived in the Endicott she rarely used the foyer because her apartment, originally servants' quarters, was accessible only by the less impressive back stairs, next to Ho's kitchen door in the alley.

They reached Ho's upstairs door and Laura heard a small whimpering sound on the other side. "Chomsky! How is the old devil?"

Ho twisted a key in the lock. "Feisty as ever. Don't let him downstairs; Mrs. Morse's corgis go crazy." He took the house key out of the leather case. "Here," he said, "take this in case you go out."

"Thank you."

They walked in and Laura bent down to let the dachshund sniff her hand. He went for her crotch instead. "Polite dog you have, Ho."

"He isn't around females much." Ho squatted to scratch Chomsky's head. "Don't sniff their crotches, sir, they find it rude." Standing, he asked, "Have you eaten, Laura?"

"No, and I'm starved."

"Then I'll fix you an apertif and appetizer, it's at least an hour before dinner."

"Just tonic and lime, please."

"But the Cinzano?"

"I don't drink enough these days to process it well. Anyway, I'm in training."

Laura went to the living room to drop off her garment bag, then back to the kitchen to be with Ho, and the food. As he sliced a lime, she opened his cabinet, singing the explanation "Crack-ers, crack-ers." Triumphantly she drew out a handful of Triscuits.

"You *are* hungry."

"I played volleyball, my man, and I'm six-feet-one. We're talking calories here, minimum thirty-eight hundred."

Laura went into the living room and stood in the bay window. Down below, the lights of evening winked around the curve of Bellingham Bay. On the bay itself a tugboat lit up like Christmas towed barges out to the south. At the city pier a Japanese freighter unloaded something Asian for the denizens of the Northwest.

Sitting on the huge leather sofa in the center of the room, Laura watched as Chomsky skittered from hassock to table to sofa in order to lie beside her. Shamelessly, he stretched his tiny legs in the air so that Laura could scratch his belly. Feeding herself Triscuits with one hand and scratching Chomsky with the other, she mulled over her options for retrieving Larry's letters. She'd be bedding down on the sofa tonight: Perhaps after Ho was asleep she could take his campus keys and slip out to the anthropology department. But what would Chomsky say to all that?

Ho came into the room and handed her the tonic with lime twist. Then he put a compact disk in the player and for a minute they listened to the crystal explosion of Vivaldi's *Four Seasons* through laser silence.

Very quietly Ho came up behind the couch and kissed Laura on the crown of her freshly shampooed head.

"Women smell so delicious. Sometimes I feel like I could squeeze one to death."

"They put you in jail for that, Ho."

"Do you want to sleep in my bed tonight? It's much more comfortable than the sofa."

"Thanks, but I'd rather stay out here."

"You needn't worry. My tests are all coming back negative. And I won't so much as sneeze on you."

"I know you wouldn't. But I'll be perfectly fine here." Laura sipped her drink.

"Too bad. I loved it when you shared my bed. Even if we didn't fuck."

"Potty mouth. But you *were* nice to curl up with."

"Do you remember the first time?"

"Sorry, I don't."

"I'll never forget. It was that awful night when my mother had just gone back to New York and I was such a wreck up there in your kitchen. You were tired from a running race and didn't want to listen to me anymore, so you just pulled me into your room, threw an arm over me and fell asleep. I've always wanted to thank you for that night."

"It was cozy, wasn't it?"

"No." Ho shook his head emphatically. "You don't understand. You have no idea how special that night was for me."

"Was it really?"

"Absolutely. You spent the night with me and weren't even interested in fucking. It was love totally removed from the act itself. It just blew my mind."

Laura sipped tonic and smiled. "All we did was fall asleep."

"There! You've done it again. Why is it that whenever we talk about this, you can't understand what I'm saying?"

"I *do* understand. But to me, it was just comforting a friend. Get it?"

"No. Chalk up one more to male-female incomprehension." Ho swirled ice cubes in his glass and began again. "I have a question, Laura. It may not seem important to you, but I've been torturing myself with it for three years now."

"Okay."

"Do you think, were it not for the horror visited upon us this age," he looked in her eyes, "do you think you would have slept with me for real back then?"

Laura gazed at him wide-eyed. "I don't know. I was certainly vulnerable enough after Larry dumped me. But, Ho, what is all this? You know perfectly well the only woman you've ever cared about is your mother."

He bristled. "You don't know that."

"I *know* that."

"Well, would you have?"

Laura put a hand to her forehead. "Ho, please don't do this to me. Not now."

"I asked a simple yes-or-no question. We both know the days when we could have been lovers is long past, so there's no threat to your health or well-being in answering. I only ask because I want to know if a woman could have ever found me attractive."

Laura sighed. "Ho, I love you dearly, but I've never wanted to sleep with you."

Ho shook his head. "I'm sorry. Juxtaposing those two phrases makes no sense to me. It's profoundly insulting."

"Try, please. I meant it kindly. Do you want me to find someplace else to stay tonight? I can."

The phone rang and as he left, Ho said, "Don't be silly. Stay right where you are."

Laura picked up the *Tribune* to read the Larry Todd article but couldn't concentrate because of the delicious coyness of Ho's telephone voice in the next room. She listened:

"But you're always bullying secretaries, it's your nature." There was a pause and he replied, "No, I don't think I can manage it tonight, I'll be busy all evening with my houseguest." A pause. "I knew you'd say that: it's a *she* and her name is Laura; she's going to sleep on my couch. Why not come over and meet her?" He paused again. "That is a bit of work. Try the O.E.D. first, then your etymology thingie. Very well, I'll talk to you tomorrow."

Laura tipped up her glass and knocked a melting ice cube into her mouth. She crunched ice, trying to control her face but the funny thought kept bending her mouth: no need to worry about Ho the Amorous anymore. He came in.

"All right, Ho. What's his name?"

"Max. He's in the theater department."

"Max Eberhardt, with the goatee?"

"It's not a goatee anymore. He's let it grow out fuller, it's very distinguished looking. He's also a boater and an art collector, quite interested in Northwest art."

"What a well-rounded sort of fellow. But tell me, how long have the two of you been an item?"

"Six months or so. I did some contextual critiques for him last summer and in the fall we started going out on his

cabin cruiser. Neither of us is taking any of this too seriously—we're much too old for that—but it is convenient having a reliable lover now that everyone's cut back so. And he's
brilliant company, really."

"A cabin cruiser. What kind?"

"A twenty-six foot Chris-Craft."

"That's so funny. I can't imagine you on a boat."

"I'll have you know that I'm quite an accomplished
boatsman. I have a yachting hat, Topsiders, everything."

"Topsiders, I love it." Laura squinted merrily at the
thought of Ho Kauffmann on a foredeck in his thick-rimmed
Topsiders. "You crack me up. When I was here I couldn't
even get you to buy running shoes. Remember I used to kid
you about your six pairs of black leather shoes?"

"And my army boots."

"I bet you asked Max if you could wear army boots on
the boat, didn't you?"

Ho looked trapped. "It would have been nice to use them
again. Well, have you ever been on a boat?"

Laura started laughing. First she grabbed her forearms to
hold herself together, then she bent over because her stomach
hurt. When she finally could speak she said, "Ho, I grew up
in Long Beach; that's like asking me if I've ever ridden in a
car."

"A subway, then? Been on a subway?"

"Touché, got me." Laura wiped a tear. "No, I can't say
I've ever ridden a subway, not even in Tokyo."

"Well, then." Ho turned on his heel and went to the
kitchen.

Laura put her feet up on the couch and once again picked
up the *Tribune*. This time she read:

SMITH ROAD WOMAN
SUBJECT OF SEARCH

Bellingham police today reported no further leads
on the whereabouts of Adele Patterson, the Whatcom
County woman missing since the May 14 shooting
death of Western University Professor Lawrence J.
Todd.

In an exclusive *Tribune* press conference today, Bellingham Police Chief Robert Ager stated that in spite of the all-points bulletin extending through nine western states and British Columbia, no traces of the 45-year-old woman have been found. Ager added that police are confident a lead will be forthcoming in the next few days.

Since the Sunday morning discovery of the 38-year-old anthropologist's shotgun death in the remote Smith Road trailer where Mrs. Patterson resides, police have conducted intensive searches involving state and local law enforcement agencies as well as the Royal Canadian Mounted Police.

The body of the associate professor of

Laura jumped off the couch and went back to the kitchen. "Ho," she called, "she's an Indian, the woman who killed Larry Todd. That makes much more sense."

"How on earth do you know she's an Indian? The *Tribune* doesn't tell us that."

"I know because 'Patterson' is one of about three last names among the Nammish out in the county. And she lives on Smith Road, near the reservation."

"But wouldn't Patterson be her married name?"

"Yes, and her first name's Adele. Adele's a really common name out there. I *know* all this, Ho. I helped the Nammish Tribal Council with their genealogy project. Every other woman was named Adele. And Patterson is *the* Nammish surname. The first white Indian agent in the 1880s was named Patterson and he had nine children by a Nammish woman."

"Point conceded, but why does it make more sense if she's an Indian?"

"Because Larry Todd ran an artifacts business on the side and he probably asked Adele Patterson to take stuff across the line for him. Nammish are the only people who have reservations on both sides of the border; they're allowed to come and go as they please. Don't you see?"

"Where did Todd get these artifacts?"

"From the bands we worked with, either Canadian or American, he didn't care. Sometimes they made new stuff, sometimes they sold old family things. Larry always carried a big duffel bag and a wad of American money. He'd buy everywhere: gas stations, bars, liquor stores. He used to say you could buy anything behind an Indian liquor store.''

''Laura, this is libelous stuff; the man was an *anthropologist*.''

''Ho, he's dead. And he probably got killed trying to get a Nammish woman to smuggle stuff across the line for him.''

''It doesn't seem very prudent of the border service to let the Nammish move freely like that.''

''Usually Nammish won't have anything to do with whites and their border games. Boy, Larry must have really done his Mr. Personality number on her.''

Ho stood very still and eyed Laura. For a full minute he would not speak.

She looked at him. ''What's the matter?''

''I'm just wondering whether you should go to the police.''

''Oh no. I don't have anything for the police. Their problem is finding Adele Patterson, and I can't help with that.''

Ho looked at her so curiously that Laura picked up one of his celery sticks and crunched it, just for the noise. She watched as he buttered French bread on the counter, waiting for her to speak the truth.

Instead she blurted out, ''How long until dinner?''

''Twenty minutes.''

''Can we walk up to campus? There's something I have to do there, and after that I can explain everything.''

Ho said nothing.

''Please, this is serious.''

''Yes, I can tell it's serious. It gets more serious by the minute.'' He looked at the kitchen clock and began fiddling with the dials on the stove. He removed the copper lid and stirred the ragout.

''Ho?''

''Yes, yes, I'll go. Just let me turn down the gas.''

They put on jackets and walked out the kitchen door into the alley. Walking through side yards of both deluxe condos and shabby student rentals, they climbed steep stairs to the redbrick campus at the top of the hill. From this height they could still see the rose tint behind Vancouver Island, last great resting place of the sun before it left town for Japan.

Laura led them past the bookstore and across the quad, finally stopping in front of the double doors of Ho's office building.

"Can you let us in?" she said.

"The building is closed to everyone but faculty after six."

"You have a key."

"Yes, to this door and to my office, but not up to the anthropology department, if that's where you want to go."

"If you let me in I can take care of everything else."

"Laura, you must tell me what you've done."

Laura shifted her weight and stared at the locked doors.

"Besides your obviously being in a lot of trouble, you've now put yourself in the position of using a friend. I don't like it one bit, and what's more, it doesn't suit you; it's not at all becoming."

"Becoming?"

"Perfectly good word, sixteenth century."

Laura turned to his waiting eyes. Sometimes she hated Ho when he used his cleverness to talk her into a corner.

"This doesn't concern you, Ho. I wrote some letters to Larry Todd and I need to get them out of his office. They're very personal and no one else has the right to read them. If you can let me in the building I can do the rest. Please."

"The offices are locked."

"I know how to get in. I won't have to break anything or do anything illegal."

Ho sighed deeply, then pulled his key case out into the light. Inserting a brass key in the lock, he turned it twice and watched Laura dart like a deer up the stairs. He went in after her and looked around.

The building was dark except for a janitor's pool of light at the end of the hall. Ho pocketed his keys and climbed wearily up the brick steps. Stepping into the second-floor corridor, he looked both ways: The only lights were Exit signs; whatever Laura was doing she did in the dark.

Ho followed blue arrows to the anthropology reception desk. The arrows pointed left, right, then around the corner. Turning at the last arrow, he stopped dead in his tracks: A shadowed Kwakiutl mask the size of a bear head stared out from a lighted display case. It scared the bejesus out of him. Recovering his wits, he walked down the hall to look for Laura. He found her in front of a metal accordion grate which sealed off the receptionist's area at night. The nine-foot grate pulled down from the ceiling and was padlocked to a bolt in the floor.

Laura had her fingers around the steel mesh and her nose resting on the lattice. Tears rolled down her face. "There's the key I need, Ho: on the wall behind the secretary's desk. I don't remember this grate being here."

Ho pulled her hands down and made her turn to face him. Putting his arms round her long strong torso, he hugged her tightly. In turn, Laura, out of habit, laid her head on the top of his and sobbed.

CHAPTER 4

Police Detective Talbot could see the most astonishing thing through the glass panel in Larry Todd's office door. Between the departmental notices and taped-up cartoons he saw a very tall, very pretty blonde rifling through the drawers. She had on a glowing ivory suit with a pencil-thin skirt and was lit with white morning from the window.

Talbot tilted his head ever so slightly to keep the moving woman in his field of vision. She was gliding around stocking-footed—entirely at home—opening and closing drawers. He watched as she pulled back a lower file drawer and began reading from a folder; she used her toe distractedly to close the drawer. Apparently unsatisfied with what she found in the folder, she climbed on the chair to reach the upper bookshelf. Her legs were amazingly long.

Stepping back to make sure the police notice was still on the door, Talbot read: KEEP OUT BY ORDER OF THE

BELLINGHAM POLICE DEPARTMENT. They hadn't used yellow tape so as not to offend the anthropologists, but the notice was right there, big as a squad car. So this woman had stolen a key and ignored an access notice: a burglar, the best-looking burglar he'd ever seen.

He peeked in again.

The woman was incredibly lovely, standing on the desk to reach a letter box. As she stretched, she tossed her yellow ponytail off her shoulder and lifted one foot for balance. Talbot stepped back and folded his arms to think.

Down the hall, a secretary in a fuzzy pink turtleneck left the reception desk and disappeared into the Xerox room. Talbot followed her. In the room he found her walking up and down the spine of a book, squashing it against the floor. She looked up at his surprised face. "They complain if their copies have gray shadows," she explained. "I was trying to flatten it out a bit."

"Who's the woman in Larry Todd's office?"

"She went in there? Am I in trouble?"

"You mean you let her in?"

The secretary pulled at her turtleneck. "When she came in this morning and asked for Dolores I figured she belonged here. I've only been here six weeks, I don't know everyone yet."

"Who's Dolores?"

"The master key. There's a tag on it that says 'Dolores.' Nobody knows who Dolores is anymore, but people use the key when they lock themselves out or forget their own keys. The woman knew about Dolores, so I figured she was someone who's been on leave. I'm really sorry, I didn't know she'd go in there."

"And you don't know who she is?"

"Never seen her before."

The secretary glanced at the office where Anthropology Chairman Terrence Buchanan was holed up with the dean of Arts and Science. Would the policeman complain to Buchanan? But Detective Talbot was already halfway down the hall. Over his shoulder he said, "When Buchanan comes out, tell him I want to see him. I'll be in Todd's office with the blonde."

Talbot stood in front of the glass pane and watched the woman reading at the desk. Not armed, he decided, and he wiped the smile off his face. Knocking three times, he listened to the surprised silence inside.

"Who is it?"

"Is Dr. Todd in?"

Talbot heard the chair roll back as she got up to open the door. "Dr. Todd has been killed, didn't you hear?"

Up close she was even lovelier. Her eyes were a cool slate-blue bracketed by thick eyebrows curling at the arches. Her mouth showed perfect white teeth and she wore pearl earrings, same as the teeth. She was almost as tall as he and she looked at him with a direct blue gaze. Wedgwood, Talbot decided, the eyes are Wedgwood blue.

Laura looked at the tall man with chocolate-brown eyes and quickly glanced away.

"What else do you know about Dr. Todd?" he asked.

Laura looked at him again, trying to think of an answer. His eyes were liquid and kind, like a cocker spaniel's. But of course, he was much taller than a cocker spaniel. She watched as he looked away, adjusted his legal pad, then look back at her. Her cheeks grew hot but she met his gaze with her best blonde-girl look. Cool, Laura, you're coolly indifferent to this man. But she could barely stop her mouth from screaming, "Six-three! He's at least six-three."

Out loud Laura said, "I'm sorry, I don't know who you are."

My God, thought Talbot, more balls than a pawnbroker. But it was time to get serious, still working hours. Talbot pulled his legal pad from under his arm and turned to a fresh page.

"Ma'am, I don't think my name's as important as yours right now. Do you mind telling me what you're doing in Dr. Todd's office?"

The blood drained from Laura's face and she went all over numb. The tall man's tone and assurance said "policeman" louder than a uniform. She had forgotten there would be police involved. Especially one so beautifully tall.

"Well?" he asked.

Laura turned to the disarray in the office. "Just a minute."

"What? I didn't hear you."

"I said, 'Just a minute.' I'm thinking."

"No." He shook his head. "I'm afraid not, ma'am. It doesn't work that way." He took her forearms and backed her up into Larry Todd's chair. "Why don't you sit down and tell me about it."

Picking up a orange plastic chair from near the door, he put it in front of her, inches from her knees. Sitting down in it, he carefully placed his feet so as not to step on her stockinged toes. Their knees were so close they almost touched. He put his legal pad in his lap and sighed loudly, waiting to hear the con she would use.

She didn't speak and after a moment he said, "What time do you have?"

She twisted her wrist, "Ten-ten."

"Fine, I'm in no hurry." He straightened his cuffs and exhaled.

Laura Ireland sat and hated this awful man. She knew the trick he was using: the closeness, the waiting. This was police intimidation and it was illegal. She'd get him for this.

"I'll sue."

"You'll what?"

"I'll sue."

Talbot tore off a sheet of paper, "Here, if you're going to sue, you'd better keep notes. You'll build a stronger case that way."

Laura folded her arms across her chest, refusing to touch the paper he had offered. It was a gesture right out of sixth grade.

Talbot sighed and looked at the blonde. "We're going to be here all day."

"And I bet you'll blame it on me."

"We could try starting all over. You know, say hello, how do you do, act like things are just perking along. I ask you some questions, maybe your name, your shoe size. Then you ask me some: 'How's the investigation?' 'Did you find Mrs. Patterson yet?' No pressure, no accusations."

Laura glared.

Talbot took the cap off his pen and looked at the legal pad.

"Your name is . . ."

"Laura Ireland."

"Laura, that's Laura with a *u*?"

"Yes."

"Very good, that's Ms. Ireland? Mrs.?"

"Laura Ireland, with an *L*."

"Absolutely, no problem. And Laura, you had business with Larry Todd?"

"He was my graduate adviser three years ago."

"Ah, much better. And could you tell me the nature of your business here in Larry Todd's office?"

"Not unless I have to."

"But it would be safe to guess that you've left something important here you've come to pick up."

"You can guess whatever you like."

"You're not telling?"

"No, but I swear it has nothing to do with the murder. I'm here about something entirely different."

"I see." As he wrote he said, "Something entirely different." He watched as hate clenched her lovely jaw and curled the tips of her long white fingers. "And just one more thing, Laura Ireland, do you have an address in town?"

"No. Yes, I'm staying with a friend."

"And her name?"

"*His* name. Dr. H. O. Kauffmann."

"Very well, Laura Ireland, did you know that entering an area posted by police is a misdemeanor punishable by fine?"

"No, I didn't know that, and I didn't know this area was posted."

"You saw the sign on the door?"

"Larry always had crazy things on his door."

"Hey, that's good. I'll have to use that at sharing time. But, since you haven't actually broken in and don't appear to have any stolen property on your person, I don't think we'll issue a citation at this time. You don't have a prior record, I assume?"

"Record?"

"No, I didn't think so."

Laura put her hands on her cheeks and looked at his pad. "And you have my name."

"Yes, I do. I couldn't let you leave without taking your name, but don't worry, it's not serious this time. Just don't go around ignoring police cordons anymore." Talbot met her eyes, stone blue and ivory, the graces on a Wedgwood vase.

There were noises in the hall and Laura recognized the booming voice of Dr. Buchanan, Bushman's father. Buchanan was using his hallway voice, his hale-fellow-well-met baritone that resonated down corridors, telling everyone that anthropology was a jolly old place to be. The voice answering Buchanan was not one she recognized. It was a low male voice so quiet she held her breath to hear it.

Buchanan's resonance and the answering purr grew closer until they were in front of Todd's door. Laura rolled the desk chair back and stood up to slip on her shoes. Talbot let her go. There was a hearty knock on the door, and after giving Laura one last look, the detective opened the door.

"Dr. Buchanan." Talbot welcomed the anthropology chairman with a hand and looked inquisitively at his colleague.

"Mr. Talbot, this is Dean Allessandro Siecetti, our dean of Arts and Sciences. The dean is here to discuss this unfortunate business with us." Buchanan saw Laura. "My dear, what a pleasant surprise. Dean Siecetti, this young lady is Miss Laura Ireland, one of our former graduate students." He extended a hand. "I wondered if you'd be joining Claudia for the tournament in Seattle." Claudia was Bushman's real name.

Dr. Buchanan had aged since Laura last saw him. Though he was still tall, with the same broad-shouldered frame as Bushman, his coarse black hair and thicket eyebrows were now peppered with gray. His jaw was slack and the drooping skin under his eyes perfectly mimicked the sagging pockets of his Harris tweed. Over the years he had learned to bend over for shorter people around him, and now, at sixty, he stood like a mid-level bureaucrat, stoop-shouldered and defeated. He put his huge hands in his pockets and stretched them taut with his wrists, his preface for speaking. "And how are things going at UCLA, Laura?"

"Very well, thank you. I turned in my last dissertation chapter before I came up to the tournament. My adviser has accepted them all so far."

Buchanan nodded knowingly to Dean Siecetti, who made no sign Buchanan existed. Dean Siecetti, in fact, was so remote he gave the impression that without six foreign languages and a Medici pedigree, a person shouldn't speak to him at all. He was nearly as tall as the rest of them, well-dressed and well-groomed, as elegant as a cello. He wore a slim-cut mohair jacket the texture of shredded tobacco and a buttery cashmere turtleneck. On his feet were burnished Italian loafers with tiny buckles and tassels.

Ignoring Buchanan, the dean turned to Laura. "Miss Ireland, how do you do. I think you have been a student of Dr. Todd's, is that right?" His voice was foreign-sounding, not so much with an accent as with odd swellings around the vowels.

"Yes, that's right, I did my master's thesis on the second level of digging at Keena Inlet. It's up in British Columbia."

"Of course, I know the place, the Tsamian Indian Reserve. The Canadian government has been an enthusiastic supporter of ours because of Dr. Todd's work. You were here with Mr. Talbot discussing something about your work, perhaps?"

Laura stared, knowing both Buchanan and Siecetti could call her bluff if she chose to lie. "No, actually, I didn't come about work; I'm really here for a much more personal reason."

"Personal?" said Talbot.

"I don't think it's a matter for the police." Laura looked at her ivory shoes, stretching the silence as long as she could.

Talbot turned to the men. "Miss Ireland and I were trying to establish what she was doing just before you arrived. I've pointed out to her that crossing a police line is a misdemeanor and that she really should be held liable. Perhaps you can get her to tell us what she's up to, I'm not having much luck myself."

Dr. Buchanan moved forward. "No, no, you must have

misunderstood, Miss Ireland will be happy to cooperate, she's an old family friend. Laura and my daughter played volleyball together, traveled all over the world—Asia, the Caribbean, Europe. Claudia wrote the most interesting letters.'' He turned to the dean, "But of course, that's not what we're talking about, is it?" He took a step over to Laura and put an arm around her shoulder.

"Laura," he looked around for support, "as an old friend, I want to assure you that no matter what you might have done in the past, we are not here to pass judgment. We realize graduate students and their advisers sometimes get very close and that maybe you and Larry Todd might have shared some of this special closeness''—he looked around to make sure he hadn't offended—''but we assure you, anything you want to say about this personal matter will be kept in the strictest professional confidence—"

"I can't assure that," said Talbot.

"Of course not. But Laura, as I was saying, you needn't feel that a direct answer to Mr. Talbot's question will in any way damage your reputation or your professional standing. That kind of thing just isn't allowed to happen these days. Am I right, Dean?"

"Of course. Almost all indiscretion can be forgiven." The dean stared coolly at Buchanan, whose grip tightened on Laura's shoulder. "Laura?" Buchanan said. He backed away and waited.

"Well, if you think it will go no farther than this room: I borrowed Dolores to get some letters that I wrote to Larry. They embarrass me now and I'd prefer that Barbara Todd not see them when Larry's papers are turned over to her."

"Yes, yes"—Buchanan nodded—"I thought as much, and I assume you didn't find your letters?"

"No."

Buchanan nodded again sympathetically.

Talbot spoke. "I have a question for Miss Ireland. Or perhaps it's better directed at you, Dr. Buchanan, since Todd was your colleague. If Todd preferred the company of graduate students—like Miss Ireland, for instance—why would his habits change so completely that he would start keeping company with a barmaid from town?"

"What?" Buchanan stretched his pockets. "Oh, I see your thinking: a change of habits. All I know about the man's habits is that he habitually appeared at the last possible moment for Monday morning classes and left Fridays at noon for Keena Inlet. But of course it appears now he didn't always go up to Keena Inlet, doesn't it?" He looked at his watch. "Why don't you ask Barbara Todd that question? She doesn't seem to mind talking about it and she'll be here very shortly."

"I've spoken with Mrs. Todd twice already and she seems to be at as big a loss as the rest of us."

Laura blurted, "I know why Larry got killed."

The three men looked at six-feet-one Laura standing in front of the window, her hair lit from behind.

"Well yes, Laura, we all know in a way," said Buchanan. "But of course, crimes of passion have a way of looking all the same after a while."

"That's not what happened at all. Adele Patterson is a Nammish tribal member, Larry was probably doing business with her."

At the word "Nammish" Talbot pushed the door shut and motioned to the desk chair.

"Miss Ireland?"

She sat down.

Talbot continued, "Although you don't realize it, you've indicated you know a great deal more about this than you should. Before you begin I should advise you that anything you say to me now can and will later—"

"Would you stop it? Of course I know a great deal about all this: I know a great deal about Larry Todd."

Talbot leaned against the desk and rubbed his forehead. "So you're telling me that Dr. Todd was more than just a paying customer of Mrs. Patterson's?"

"Oh dear Lord." Buchanan sat down in the orange chair. "A paying customer? She's not a prostitute, is she?"

"All kinds of rumors are floating around. We intend to follow up all of them. Miss Ireland, if you mean to indicate they moved drugs across the line together, are you willing to come down and tape a statement? I assume we're talking Vancouver now."

"Not drugs, the Nammish won't have anything to do with whites and their drugs, they never have."

"What then?"

"Indian artifacts."

Talbot pulled back his head in disbelief. "Like in the tourist shops?"

"No, like in museums. Like the Berlin Museum show last year. It didn't look anything like a tourist shop. Of course, some people might have thought so."

"Laura." Dr. Buchanan gave her a pleading look.

Dr. Siecetti, who had been standing with his arms behind his back, took out a handkerchief and pressed the edges gently around his nose. "Miss Ireland, what you say Dr. Todd did, this artifact buying, this is a serious charge. Anthropologists must be above marketplace values."

"Dean," said Buchanan, "I don't think Laura really means everything she says about Dr. Todd. She left here feeling very angry with him"—he nodded to Laura—"as she had every right to be."

"I'm sorry to disappoint you, Dr. Buchanan, but I watched Larry Todd illegally buy all kinds of Kwakiutl art when I was here. If I had to guess at what was going on I'd say that Larry was using Adele Patterson to move stuff across the line for him; that was always his biggest problem, getting artifacts past Canadian customs."

Detective Talbot seemed sad. "Miss Ireland, I'm going to have to ask you to come in for questioning. Your information is the first we've heard about smuggling."

"Then you've been asking the wrong people. And I'm not going any place with you. You'll have to do something official—arrest me—to get me in. Even if you do, I couldn't tell you any more. Have you talked to the people who dealt with Larry regularly, his graduate students, the Tsamians?"

"Laura, please."

"Dr. Buchanan, he hasn't even done his homework and he wants to take me in."

Dr. Siecetti spoke. "You seem to know a great deal about this business. Perhaps you have some idea where these artifacts might be, Miss Ireland?"

"Adele Patterson must have them someplace; but as for where she is, I wouldn't know." She turned to Talbot. "You've asked the Nammish?"

"Yes."

"Then I can't help you. Find Adele Patterson and you'll find the artifacts. Now if you'll please excuse me, I don't think I should be here if Barbara is coming." Laura went to the door.

"Miss Ireland," said Dean Siecetti, "if there is any way I can help you while you're visiting our campus, please let me know."

"Thank you. I will." Laura smiled genially at the dean, deliberately ignoring Talbot.

"Where are you going?" asked Talbot.

"Some friends are waiting for me in the gym," she said.

Talbot let her go but spoke to her retreating back. "That's a lovely suit for gymnasium wear, Miss Ireland. Will I be able to find you there later?"

"Maybe, maybe not. But thank you for the compliment."

After Laura had turned into the stairwell, Talbot looked at the waiting academics. "I think she's actually answered all my questions, Dr. Buchanan. I wanted to ask you who else I should interview and she mentioned the Tsamian Indians in British Columbia and Todd's graduate students. Can you think of anyone else?"

"You said you've already seen Barbara Todd . . ."

"Yes, and I am supposed to see her again this afternoon about an insurance waiver. Maybe I can talk with her now if she's coming here."

Buchanan looked at his watch again and then out the window to the quad. "Yes, there she is." He stayed watching at the window and Siecetti spoke abruptly, "Gentlemen, I think I should take my leave. Mr. Talbot, it was a pleasure meeting you. I wish you good luck with your investigation." He extended a hand. "As I told Miss Ireland, let me know if I can assist you in any matter."

"Thank you."

Talbot walked over to the window with Buchanan to watch Barbara Todd. He spotted the widow easily—a bulky woman in her late thirties striding across the quad in cowboy boots and a knitted brown poncho. On her head was a red beret. As they watched her Buchanan asked, "You had no problem confirming Barbara's whereabouts over the weekend, did you? At this point, she deserves as little grief as possible."

"I'm afraid I can't discuss that with anyone but Mrs. Todd."

"Of course not, excuse me."

In a moment they heard the clomping boots on the stairs and an echoing voice in the stairwell. ". . . take my stuff out of the display case I know a woman who'll give me eight hundred dollars for the Tlingit blanket."

Buchanan went out in the hall to meet her and Talbot followed, locking the office door behind him.

"Barbara, you know Detective Talbot."

Barbara Todd stared at Talbot and said curtly, "I've got the insurance form." She pulled the red beret off her hair, revealing a gray streak that started at her forehead and disappeared into the long brown braid down her back.

"We need to talk about that."

Buchanan interrupted by maneuvering Barbara over to the hallway display case and parking her in front of it. "See what I was telling you? Your things give a wonderful context to the Kwakiutl mask, don't you think?"

"They certainly do."

"And they make such a good impression on visitors. You can't be persuaded to keep them here?"

"Fat chance. I already know what I'm going to do with the blanket and baskets. I might even wear the jewelry."

"Very well, I'll get the key. Perhaps while I'm gone Detective Talbot can change your mind by telling you how nice it all looks."

Buchanan left and Barbara said to Talbot again, "I've got the insurance form."

"Yes, and I won't be able to sign it just yet."

"But I wrote down everything I did this weekend. Isn't that what you wanted?"

"I'm having a little problem with part of it."

"Which part?"

"The bridge game Saturday night."

"Then call Ed and Felicity Peacock. Matter of fact, Felicity is upstairs in the English department right now. Go up and ask her; she can even tell you what I ate."

"I've spoken with the Peacocks. And they referred me back to you."

"What about?"

"They were reluctant to mention who the fourth player was. I'm assuming you were a foursome."

"But they did tell you I was over there, didn't they?"

"Yes."

"Well then, what does it matter who else was there?"

"We think it matters a great deal."

"Our fourth was a 'he' and I'm not really seeing him publicly right now. You understand?"

"You've been seeing him for a while, then?"

"Yes. But it has nothing to do with Larry's death. When it came time, I was prepared to divorce Larry; he wasn't the greatest husband, as you've probably figured out."

Talbot exhaled. "I'll have to get back to you later."

"I can't wait forever."

Buchanan arrived with the key, so Talbot excused himself. Standing in the stairwell, he finished his notes, then walked down the brick steps to the first-floor lobby. In the corner, the anthropology secretary was waiting for him. She picked at her fuzzy pink collar and glanced nervously up the stairs to make sure Talbot was alone.

"Well hello," Talbot said.

"I thought of something else I should tell you." She let out words in little bursts, as if she was afraid to let them go. "That blonde wasn't the only one who's borrowed Dolores to go through Dr. Todd's office."

"Who else?"

"Dr. Buchanan took Dolores Monday morning, after we heard about Dr. Todd. Later I saw him coming out of Dr. Todd's office. I'm almost sure he was carrying something."

"You don't know what it was?"

"No, but if you have to ask him, could you not say who told you? I just got this job six weeks ago."

"I'll make it sound like I heard it from a faculty member."

"Another thing: The blonde was very chatty this morning. She asked all kinds of questions about Dr. Todd and Barbara. I bet she could really clear up a lot of this."

Talbot's eyes rested on the secretary. "I bet she could too."

CHAPTER 5

Detective Talbot never could figure out why they called it the unmarked police car. Everybody in town recognized the chromeless Detroit hog—schoolchildren even waved. Pulling it up in front of the Fat Cat Tavern, he parked close to the curb. There was no off-street parking at the Fat Cat because the tavern was built out on pilings, right next to the Indian fishing docks. Sometimes it was hard keeping the lid on things at the Fat Cat: lots of split lips, lots of drunks going into the bay.

Talbot stood in the doorway and squinted until he saw the stocky dark figure of Charlie Washington at the end of the bar. Charlie wiped his hands on his apron and motioned to Talbot to join him on the stools.

"Been expecting you," he said. "Sorry I wasn't here the other day."

"How was Reno?"

"Wife hit a jackpot on the bandits. Me, I should have stayed home." Light from the doorway sculpted the acne scars on Charlie's cheeks. It caught the sheen of his neatly combed black hair and the stainless steel keyminder attached to his belt. Under his bartender's apron he wore a black necktie.

Talbot said, "Sorry about what we did to your lockers back there. The guys had trouble getting the cutters on."

"You guys think you'd find a shotgun or something? I can't imagine Shugie even picking one up."

"Shugie?"

"Shugie Patterson, Adele Patterson, same difference. She likes people to call her Shugie."

Talbot wrote down the name at the top of his legal pad and put a foot on the barstool rung. "Okay, you know what I'm here for, want to get started?"

"Sure."

"First question: Your full name is . . ."

"Charlie Twofeather Washington."

"And you are a Lummi tribal member?"

"I am enrolled in both the Suamish and the Nammish tribes."

"And how would you describe your occupation?"

"I am the owner of the Fat Cat Tavern."

"For?"

"Nine years."

"And how long had your trip to Reno been planned?"

"Two months. Boy, you guys don't fool around, do you? Two months. My wife made the reservation through Kulshan Travel, you can check that out. Sunday through Tuesday gets you the cheapest rates."

"So you last saw Adele at work Saturday night?"

"That is correct."

"Can you remember anything she said or did that would help explain her subsequent disappearance?"

"Her what?"

"Did she say or do anything that would help explain her disappearance?"

"Look, I'm really not good at this kind of speaking. Can't we just talk about it?"

"Sure, go ahead."

"Now what did you ask?"

"We were at the part where Adele came to work Saturday night but not on Sunday afternoon."

"That's right, she didn't show up for her shift Sunday and we couldn't get her on the phone."

"You weren't concerned?"

"They all miss shifts sometimes, always have an excuse. Shugie's got a lot going on."

"Like what?"

"Oh, projects, workshops at the Holiday Inn, psychology and stuff. She really likes psychology."

"She in therapy or something?"

"Oh no, she's fine. A little dumb but basically she's fine. Psychology is an interest of hers, you know? Really gets the customers going on it: Reads palms, does horoscopes, nutrition, tells the guys how they should eat out on the boats. It's kind of fun. She made me change to unsalted peanuts in here." Charlie pushed over a bowl of nuts. "If she did kill that professor, something was really wrong. I can barely imagine her doing it."

"Got any ideas where she might have run off to?"

Charlie shrugged. "She's got a sister in Canada, ex-husband in Alaska. She said she wanted to go back to school sometime—get her GED and go to college." Charlie slapped the bar, amused. "Maybe she went to college."

"She say where?"

"I was just kidding, she can't go back to school. My personal opinion is that she's too disorganized to ever do something like that. And then, Shugie never can get ahead with money."

"Money problems?"

"Not problems, not that bad."

"What then?"

Charlie looked around the room for inspiration. His eyes took in the black-framed photos of fishing boats on the wall. They examined the gleaming twelve-foot mahogany bar that was his pride and joy. "Okay," he said, "on payday she sits on that stool and pays bills from her purse. She keeps everything—bills, letters, coupons—in this big purse she carries.

Calls it her office. By the time she finishes writing checks for the bills she barely has enough for groceries. I pay the girls good—going wage plus some—so I don't think it's my fault. No matter how much I pay her, Shugie just finds ways to spend it. I stopped worrying about her long time ago.''

"What kind of stuff does she buy?"

"Just regular stuff: appliances at the health food store—a juicer, you know? Flowers for her friends, oh, a singing telegram once—that was thirty-five dollars. Her phone bills are always high, higher than mine. A reducing machine—she sold that. Lots of shoes. She never can find a pair that fits right—but those girls are on their feet all night long."

"Who does she call with those big phone bills?"

"Her husband in Alaska."

"They're divorced."

"I think they both get kind of lonely sometimes, you know?"

Talbot scribbled "phone bills" on his legal pad and framed the question about Shugie's other occupation.

"Charlie, what kind of guys go out to the trailer with Shugie? Any regulars? Somebody who'd get jealous?"

Charlie sat up straight on the stool. "I've been thinking about that too, but I don't know. She doesn't do that too much anymore. And even when she does, it's not anything too serious. You know, more like a joke."

"A joke?"

"I swear it's not that big a deal. Shugie can't ever be a real hooker. She's okay-looking and everything, and the extra weight don't look bad, but she doesn't know from meat loaf what the hell she's doing, from what the guys tell me."

"Charlie, the work isn't that hard."

"No, you don't get it. With Shugie it's like she'll start trying to take care of you, you know? The guys say right away they can tell not to get too serious, like she'll start calling you at work or something. Most of the regulars went out there once or twice, then they saw what the deal is and won't go anymore. Sometimes she gets guys from Alaska, or roadies from California. But I already said, she don't do it much anymore."

"Charlie, I just sent the lab the biggest pile of sex shit I've ever seen."

"Oh that stuff, that don't mean nothing. Shugie orders it from catalogs. She doesn't know how to use it, she takes it out for a laugh."

A commotion was developing back in the kitchen. Charlie looked back, then turned around to answer Talbot. "Look, don't misunderstand about Shugie, this is a nice place here, like a family. My wife does my books and she knows about Shugie. All the wives do. If the wives wanted her out"—he jerked his thumb for emphasis—"she'd be gone in a flash. They don't care, so she stays. It's sort of fun, like a sideshow. Not like a sideshow; she's a real nice girl."

Talbot wrote "Alaska residents" and "California transients" and tried again: "One more time, can you think of anything she did or said Saturday, maybe before, that would help us determine where she is right now?"

"Like I said, she was acting completely normal. My personal opinion is that Shugie couldn't kill anybody."

"We always like personal opinions."

"And there's something else I wanted to say to you after you guys came in here and banged up my lockers: I don't mind you tearing up my property like that but when you find Shugie, don't go treating her like garbage, you hear? She works for me, and she's a citizen, just like anyone else."

"Charlie, let me tell you something. We don't treat anybody like garbage, even though some of them sure smell like it."

The door banged several times back in the kitchen and each time it opened they heard agitated voices. Talbot said, "If you need to ride herd on the kitchen help, go ahead. I'll finish up my notes."

"They'll call me if they need me." As Charlie spoke a bartender came out of the kitchen and stood beside the varnished mahogany slab.

"What's the matter, Johnny?"

The bartender looked past his boss toward Talbot. "Maybe you better come see what they found out under the dock."

•   •   •

Of the two kinds of geeks who bother women runners—car geeks and foot geeks—Laura preferred the geeks in cars. Take the one who was following her now in the boulevard bike lane. No way on God's green earth would he ever leave his rolling security, and she could lose him anytime she chose by breaking out for unpaved territory.

Ahead to the right was a stairway down to Bayside Park. Laura ran past it, waited for the geek to drive by, then cut back to the stairs. Down in the park she could hear the geek revving his engine on the boulevard, deciding whether to follow. She knew he wouldn't.

Laura liked running near salt water. The oxygen quality was high enough to eat, all that high-class plankton dancing around in the sun.

The geek was back. He had driven his car down the service road and was waiting for her at the far end of the seawall. She would have to run past him or veer away again. What the hell, she was here first. She ran toward him.

Surprise! The geek started to get out of his car. She ran past in silence and Detective Talbot fell in beside her.

"How far we going?" he asked.

"Couple of miles."

"That's good, I'm not going to last too long in street shoes."

"You don't have to run."

"Sure I do, or else I'd have to stop you to talk and I know better than to try that."

"Well hurray, Mr. Talbot learned something useful this morning."

"You don't know my first name."

"And there's no reason to learn it, is there?"

"Fair enough." Their feet hit the sidewalk stride for stride. In a moment he said, "Say, I checked out the friend you're staying with. He's quite an interesting fellow, forty-three-years old, never married—"

"If you mean to say he's gay, go ahead, this is the twentieth century."

"Gay's cool, but it seems he runs with a pretty fast crowd—artists, architects, lawyers. They do a lot of shuttling back and forth between Vancouver and Seattle."

''Ho Kauffmann has a lot of friends.''

''It appears he does.''

''That's what you wanted to tell me, Ho is fast-lane?''

''Wish you weren't so flip. Do you really know how Ho Kauffman spends his time?''

''As a matter of fact, I do. He reads and translates about twelve hours a day. To relax he polishes his shoes.''

''You weren't here last winter.''

''No.''

''Hear about his Christmas party?''

''No, and I don't want to. I don't like gossip.'' Laura picked up the pace, out of spite, but Talbot seemed to like it faster.

The seawall walk petered out to a gravel path which wound through a littered shoreline of blackberry vines and rusting metal. Talbot dropped behind and they ran silently, concentrating on their footing.

After a minute he called, ''The largest salmon cannery in the world was on this site.''

''You didn't come here to talk archaeology, did you?''

''No, I came here to ask about some information you supplied that's costing the department a lot of money. I'm supposed to make sure we've got it right.''

''I supplied?''

''Yeah. Just a minute.''

They came out of the blackberries onto gravel beach. Again he fell in by her side.

''Well?'' Laura asked.

''You said when we found Adele Patterson she'd have a duffel bag of Indian artifacts with her.''

''You found her?''

''Never mind about her just yet. These artifacts we're supposed to find, tell me what's worth taking out of Canada that way.''

''Plenty of things: fish clubs, daggers, weavings, sometimes even larger ceremonial pieces—masks, rattles, blankets.''

''Who buys the stuff?''

''Art lovers. Northwest art appeals to a lot of people, it's very high-sensibility stuff.''

"You going to tell me what that means?

"That means the objects are both spiritual and intellectual; that when you stand back and ask what gives the objects their aesthetic power the answer is that they were created by an acutely conscious people with a sense of reverence for their spot on the planet, this 'edge of nowhere' we're presently running through. In strict usage you could even say that Northwest art is religious art since coastal people ritualized many of their everyday events and created their everyday objects as vehicles of ritualization. Am I boring you?"

"This morning you mentioned a museum show in Berlin."

"Yes, it's really brought a lot of attention to the Pacific Northwest."

"And I assume that jacked prices up?"

"How do you know about that?"

"Do you know Ralph Thomas at the museum?"

"Of course."

"Interesting guy, had lunch with him. He explained that international art world was really quite a small pond, everybody knowing everyone's business. Said when news breaks internationally about a new exhibition being mounted somewhere, dealers swoop down beforehand to buy up all the lookalike pieces. Like insider trading."

"But it's not entirely museums and dealers pushing up prices. My adviser said that when investment counselors said to go forth and diversify last year, a lot of people who couldn't afford Picassos and gold went into so-called third world art. He said he even saw a Haida mask in an apartment on the Île St. Louis. That's in Paris."

"Behind the cathedral. So essentially we're talking about a nickel-and-dime way to pick up assets?"

"I don't know about the nickel-and-dime stuff, to me the markup is unbelievable. You know those bentwood cooking boxes that Indians make from one long plank?"

"Yes."

"I saw a Japanese man pay seven hundred and fifty dollars for one in the Seattle airport shop and Larry used to pay forty to sixty dollars for them. He would kill to get his hands on one of those."

"Would he?"

"Figure of speech." An edge crept into Laura's voice. "You haven't told me about Adele Patterson. I bet you caught her coming back to her trailer to pick up her clothes."

"Wrong, but you have a lawman's head: We do have the sheriff watching the roads out there." He ran along, saying nothing else.

"She didn't have artifacts with her?"

"That's what we're trying to find out."

"I don't get it."

"When we found Adele Patterson, she was facedown under a pier."

Laura stopped and looked at him, but he kept running. She caught up and said, "Here in town?"

"Behind the Fat Cat where she worked. We've got divers in the water now and that's costing money. They're mostly looking for a shotgun but I told the chief we should be looking for a duffel bag too."

"She was shot?"

"No, looks like a drowning. Probable concussion in the upper right parietal, body wrapped in tire chains."

"Parietal's one of the head plates . . ."

"Back of the head, right side. Means she was hit from the rear by a right-handed person taller than herself. Since she was five-two that profiles most of the adult population."

"I even fit that profile."

"Yeah."

They ran in silence a minute, then Laura asked, "So why are your divers looking for a shotgun?"

"Larry Todd was shot with one Saturday night, remember? We're wondering if the murderer dumped his shotgun the same time he hit on Patterson."

"Are you saying Adele Patterson didn't shoot Larry?"

"Looks like a third party is involved, wouldn't you say?"

"But who would kill both of them? Her husband?"

"Ex-husband. We've been told he's in Alaska till the end of crab season."

Ahead was a sandstone outcropping that jutted into the bay. Waves lapped one side and a footpath ran to the top. Laura tucked her head and ran straight up the knoll with

Talbot close behind. Halfway up he said, "Stop at the top, I have to ask a question before we can go any farther." They climbed panting to the top. On the crest Laura bounced up and down, taking deep breaths and jogging in place.

"Hold still, I have to ask you something," he said.

"I don't want to cool off yet."

"I said hold still."

"Okay." Laura wiped her face and looked at the detective. His blue oxford shirt was sticking to the flat spot between his pectorals and he had on no undershirt. He wiped his forehead with his sleeve and untucked the rest of his cotton shirt. A clean laundry smell rose up with his body heat and Laura saw the muscle tone on his pecs. Talbot looked at her with his liquid brown gaze and asked, "Have you ever used a shotgun before?"

"That's the one that slams your shoulder out of the socket, isn't it?"

"You've shot one?"

"I guess. I can't remember where though."

"Then I have a second question. Where were you Saturday night?"

"What is this? I thought you were going to ask something important. I was home, in Los Angeles, working on my dissertation."

"Saturday night?"

"Obviously you've never been in graduate school."

"False. Do you have witnesses?"

"For Saturday? No, but I turned in a whole dissertation chapter Monday."

Talbot shook his head. "I'd like it better if you could firm up some witnesses for the weekend."

"You'd like it better? God, you've got nerve." She resented terribly that his pecs were toned and he smelled of clean clothes. "I'd like it better if you'd run off a pier."

"We already knew that, didn't we?" Talbot went to the edge of the knoll to run down, then turned back to Laura. "About your friend Dr. Kauffmann. What we know about people who move stuff over the line is that once they've found a way past customs, usually they don't care what it is they move."

"Ho's not moving stuff."

"I've just stated a general principle for you, okay? And one more thing: Every time I turn around someone mentions your name in connection with Larry Todd. I don't want you leaving town without getting permission from my department, do you understand?" He ran down the path to the beach.

When he was out of earshot Laura answered him, "Right, fellow," and she watched him run toward the park. Detective Talbot didn't keep his feet near the ground like a distance runner. His stride was stretched-out and slightly profligate and he held his chest high and still. A middle-distance runner, she guessed, which was unfortunate: Middle-distance was her favorite, and she was looking for reasons to hate Detective Talbot.

She stood on the knoll a full fifteen minutes, waiting for the sweat to dry and her breathing to quiet. Out on the water, sunlight sparkled in the dance of the day. Farther still, contours of smoky islands gave promise of blue shade.

Laura took the deep sighing breath of exercise and turned to run down the knoll. Suddenly a pop of noise made a sharp sensation shoot across her upper arm. She grabbed her triceps and looked to the boulevard cliff, from where the sound had come. Around her feet the ground exploded with stinging gravel; it was inconceivable, but someone on the cliff was shooting at her. She dropped to the ground and skaddled backward to the safe side of the outcropping. Again she heard the popping of a gun.

Holding her upper arm Laura lay on her back calling to the sky. "Mr. Talbot! Mr. Talbot!" Some cop. Lots of help he was. She yelled again; then the horror crossed her mind: What if Mr. Talbot was shooting? But that didn't make any sense. She stopped yelling and just looked at the sky. She felt a frightening need to see all that was really there: cumulus, blue, white, gull, gray.

Laura's arm began to throb and she twisted the muscle around to take a look. A thin streak of red flesh ran across her skin. In the streak tiny swells of blood were rising to the surface. She flexed the arm and found it worked. A flesh wound. Rolling on her stomach she snaked over to the side of the outcropping to peak around.

On the cliff behind the beach, the woods were perfectly still where ragged smoke clouds were lifting from the undergrowth. Nothing moved. Laura lay still, watching for a very long time.

After a while, a woman with a leashed terrier came down the path from the seawall. Laura rose and walked the steep hills back to Ho's. Behind the door she found Chomsky agitated and pacing, his long nails tapping staccato against the wood floors. "Ho?" she called, but he was still up on campus. Quickly she went to the bathroom and covered the raw forearm flesh with four Band-Aids laid sideways. Then she sat on Ho's bed to wait. But actually, Ho would be almost as bad as Detective Talbot—no help at all.

Putting on warm-ups, Laura let herself out the kitchen door and jogged the alley stairways up to campus. Sweating and out of breath, she entered the administration building and walked into the reception area for the dean of Arts and Science. The secretary looked up. She was a healthy-looking brunette with a race-walking trophy on her desk.

"May I see Dean Siecetti?" Laura asked.

Scanning her appointment dairy, the secretary set her face for a professional lie. "The dean is in a meeting now and won't be back until a—there he is." She looked past Laura's shoulder and smiled. Laura turned around to see Dean Siecetti entering, a sheaf of file folders under his arm.

"Miss Ireland,"—he bowed slightly—"what a pleasant surprise." His face turned grave. "But I hope your visit doesn't mean that things are amiss with you."

"May I see you privately, please?" she asked.

"Certainly." To the secretary he said, "Penny, no calls, please."

Closing the door behind them, he motioned Laura to a chair by the desk. "What is it?"

Laura unzipped her jacket and bared her shoulder. Peeling back the mat of Band-Aids, she said, "I've been shot."

Siecetti leaned forward and examined the scratch. "Are you in pain? Who did this? You must call the police." He reached for the telephone.

"No, don't do that. That's the problem. I think it was Detective Talbot who shot at me."

Siecetti looked somberly at her arm. Putting down the phone receiver, he contemplated the enormity of what she said. From the desk blotter he picked up a fat gold fountain pen. Distractedly he rubbed the gold fluting with his thumbs. "If this is so, you have created quite a problem for us. The next question, of course, is whether Detective Talbot is acting on his own or whether he is in consortium with someone else." He looked directly at her, trying to inject some humor. "I choose not to believe it is the entire Bellingham police that conspires against you." The lilting voice was like a balm. Laura smiled weakly.

Smoothing down the Band-Aids, she zipped up her jacket and said, "I don't think the entire department is against me either."

"But what do you consider Detective Talbot's motives to be?"

"I don't know. I just met him this morning. Then he came to talk to me while I was running in the park"—she motioned to her clothes—"and then a few minutes after he left, somebody shot at me."

"Very well." Siecetti placed the pen neatly across the top of his blotter. "This must be acted on immediately. Let me call some people downtown to see what we can find out about Detective Talbot. But what are your immediate plans?"

"Well, I'd like to take a bus down to my volleyball tournament in Seattle. I play again tomorrow morning."

"A good idea, I think. Meanwhile I suggest you tell no one about what's happened until I investigate further. Will your teammates ask you about your arm?"

"I can hide it. We have long sleeves."

"Very good. Is it hurting you now? Do you need some medication?"

"It's throbbing a little. I'll take aspirin if it really bothers me."

"You're lucky the wound is superficial."

"I know."

There seemed nothing else to say, so Laura stood up.

Siecetti stood too. "I'm so sorry this happened. I feel somehow that the college is responsible."

"No, it's not your fault at all."

As a parting, Siecetti added, "And if you have any other thoughts about Dr. Todd, the smuggling—anything—please don't hesitate to call."

"Thank you. You've been a big help."

His brow wrinkled with concern. "Please be cautious, Miss Ireland."

"I will. Good-bye."

CHAPTER 6

Talbot parked the big black LTD next to the stolen bicycle fleet in City Hall's basement. Still sitting in the car, he began filling in his clipboard. When he looked up, the desk clerk from upstairs was standing by the car door.

"Don't even get out," she said. "The boat's been waiting two hours." She handed him a "While You Were Out."

Talbot read: *Visitor's Dock, Jolly Roger, Barry Cunliffe.* "Betty, what's this?"

"I assume Barry Cunliffe is one of *the* Cunliffes and he's sent a boat over because he wants to talk to you. He was a panic on the telephone, said he was a graduate student of Larry Todd's and wants to make his position perfectly clear."

"Is that right?" Starting up the LTD again, Talbot backed out into the daylight and pointed the massive hood in the direction of the docks.

The *Jolly Roger* wasn't hard to find. She was a red twenty-four-foot Bayliner flying a private burgee. Talbot would have laughed out loud except that the skipper was a weather-beaten little man who looked embarrassed to be seen on the thing. Walking down the ramp, Talbot eyed the skipper. "Barry Cunliffe?"

"Barry's at home; I work for his father. Come aboard, Barry's waiting for you." He started the engines and piloted the *Jolly Roger* out past the breakwater and down the length of Bellingham Bay. The light chop on the water fluted gray and white under afternoon clouds. On the eastern hillside, painted frame houses looked out to the flat western arm of the bay and to the jagged peaks of Vancouver Island beyond.

The skipper piloted casually with a forefinger on the wheel, and after passing through gulls and fishermen at the tide rip, decided to be friendly. Over the engine noise he called to Talbot, "Saw an ambulance at the Fat Cat today. Indian?"

"Don't know," Talbot said. The skipper looked incredulous and moved a step away.

Rounding the south end of Lummi Island, the skipper pulled out into the Vancouver shipping channel and wove gingerly between a freighter and a tug. When he plunged through the cut leading into the more tranquil San Juan Islands, Talbot lost his bearings. "Which island we going to?"

"Pickett."

"I don't know that one."

"Old-timers call it War Island and the chart's got it as Cannery Island. Cunliffes got it from the Pickett side of the family, so they call it Pickett Island."

"Why do I know the Cunliffes' name?"

"Canneries? Or maybe you're thinking of old-time railroading."

"That's right. It was a Cunliffe got one through here, wasn't it?"

"Here, and lots of other places. Vancouver to Seattle was just one of his little projects. The big ones were getting tracks into some of those copper mines in Alaska."

"Cunliffes didn't start in railroads, did they? I remember something about big lumber tracts."

"Oh yeah, lumber too. Old Man Cunliffe—Barry's great-grandfather—patented a process to pressure-treat fir timbers for railroad ties. Sold his own lumber back to the railroad contractors. Made a lot of money back then. No taxes either.''

The Bayliner wove through the green San Juan Islands, the 1859 scene of the "Pig War," the last real estate dispute between America and England. The bigger San Juans were dream islands—lush forested parcels subdivided for the rich and retired. The small islands were more like nightmares—barren outcroppings white-stained by gulls, treacheries for navigators, disappointments for developers.

For the better part of an hour they motored between islands, admiring both scenery and residences. After a quick run through the rocks off Canoe Island, the *Jolly Roger* swung north around a sandstone point to enter a broad gray cove. Half the cove was dotted with an ancient grid plan of rotten pilings. "Old cannery docks," the skipper shouted, and he swung the boat toward clear water. On the rise above the cove was a sprawling fieldstone lodge with mullioned windows and a dozen chimneys. Bays and balconies jutted from the walls and showy gardens spilled down to the slender beach. A mock Tudor boathouse anchored the gardens to the cove.

The skipper pulled up to the boathouse dock and cut the engine. "Barry's waiting for you up at the house." He held up a spray can with a cone attachment. "When you're ready to leave, come down and use this air horn. I'll take you home." He disappeared up the hill.

Talbot climbed off the boat to see two German shepherds barking joyfully down the wide stone steps from the house. The dogs were eager and playful and looking for a friend. Behind them came a soft pudgy man in his early thirties. His brown hair was freshly cut and his pale jowly face was as smooth as a child's. He called back the dogs, who ignored him. Smiling his way down the steps, he held out a polite hand to Talbot. "Now tell me again who you are?"

"I don't think we've ever met."

"Excuse me, I'm Barry. Your department said they'd be sending someone over and I didn't get the name."

"Talbot, Bellingham P.D."

"How do you do. Down, Winston, down. This isn't very neighborly, is it? Let's go up to the house and I'll make us some daiquiris. Dinner can be anytime."

"No daiquiris on duty, and I had hoped to be back in time for dinner."

"Oh." Barry's soft mouth pursed in disappointment. "I was hoping you could stay the evening." He started toward the house, gesturing for Talbot to follow. "I thought you might enjoy a tour; most of our visitors do. Sometimes they even find artifacts at our Indian battle site in Little Cove."

"Is there some misunderstanding? I thought you had something to tell me about Larry Todd."

"Everything to tell you." Barry urged him forward. "I'm the person who got Larry Todd started in Northwest culture. If I hadn't introduced him to the Tsamians he'd still be working on Winnebagos. Isn't that the most ridiculous name?"

The dogs nipped at Talbot's ankles. Spying a nasty rubber ball in the flower bed, he stooped to sling it down the lawn. The joyful shepherds ran after it. Talbot turned to his host, "Barry, what do you want?"

"Want? I don't want anything." He took Talbot's arm conspiratorily. "As a matter of fact, I have something important to tell you—about myself and Barbara Todd. But it's all very circular and I'm afraid I'm not accustomed to dealing curtly with important things. Please come up an have a beverage. We can talk about it."

Talbot started walking again.

Satisfied with his prize, Barry led Talbot across the summer lawn and through wide doors to the dining room. Pushing back a swinging kitchen door, he said to an unseen presence, "We need a tray, please. Nothing alcoholic." He motioned Talbot into a huge living room anchored to the earth by a massive stone hearth.

The living room was decorated as a library, lined with glass-fronted hardwood shelves holding leather-bound books, handwoven baskets, and Indian masks. Talbot's attention was drawn to the ceiling beams, where a full-sized Indian war canoe hung from brass chains. Chinked out with hand tools from one huge cedar log, the graceful twelve-man boat began at a high jutting bowsprit, bowed wide at midships, then tapered again to a tiny flattened stern. Still visible was the dimpled pattern of adz marks covering the outer hull.

Cunliffe said, "Impressive, isn't it? Great-grandmother's family found it at Little Cove when they came here in the 1880s. We believe it to be Haida since they often came down from Canada on slave raids. Our cows used to use it for a drinking trough; isn't that awful?"

"You bet."

A plain woman in a cotton housedress shuffled in with a tray of drinks. Acknowledging neither Barry nor Talbot, she put the tray on a table and left.

Talbot looked over the selection. "Seltzer, please."

"Very good."

"How do you know the Tsamians?" asked Talbot. "They're pretty far north, aren't they?"

Before answering, Barry indicated that Talbot should sit on an oak-framed Mission sofa that faced the hearth. He seated himself in a matching chair padded with worn cushions of indeterminate-colored leather. "I've spent every summer since my childhood boating around the inland passage," he said. "I know every lumber camp, every hot spring, every Indian settlement from here to Alaska. I know the Northwest coast like the back of my hand. Both past and present."

Talbot took a sip. "Then maybe you can tell me the problem with library information on the tribes."

"What do you mean?"

"I need to get a handle on Tsamians, Nammish, and a few of the others and all I can find are dusty old books about Kwakiutl potlatching customs."

"Oh God, you've found the Boas. That man has done more damage . . ." Barry began again. "The reason all the scholarly information is on the old Kwakiutl potlatch is that Franz Boas came up here around the turn of the century and hung out with the coastal tribes in Canada. He, along with everyone else, was fascinated with the huge giveaways of material goods associated with potlatchs; they just didn't know what to make of it. The end result of their research, as Larry Todd used to point out, is that it tells you more about what was important to the researchers than to the Kwakiutl."

"Did Larry Todd dig in your cove too?"

"Heavens no. I never let anyone else near our cove; I matriculated under Larry Todd so that I could come back and do our cove professionally."

"So how's work going?"

Barry's face showed annoyment. "I'm not actually working at the moment. I've started once or twice, but archaeology is incredibly painstaking work; one needs to be surrounded with the right people to really do it right. That's one of the reasons I've been in contact with Barbara Todd."

"Barbara's coming over here to help you with the cove?"

"In a manner of speaking. I'm coming to that. First you need to understand how talented Barbara is in her own right. In my opinion she is definitely more gifted than Larry ever was. She's the one who worked so hard at ingratiating Larry with the Tsamians after I introduced them."

"So you and Barbara have made a pact to do archaeology together now."

"But only after a decent interval. At present I'm limited to dropping in on her whenever I'm in Bellingham."

"You mean you aren't a graduate student right now?"

"Has there been some misunderstanding? I told the woman in your office that I *was* a graduate student of Larry's. I haven't been in school in at least four years."

"I see. So now you just keep up with Barbara?"

"Well, I certainly wasn't interested in keeping up with her husband."

"Not your favorite guy, huh?"

Barry's mouth tightened. "I wouldn't treat my dogs the way he treated Barbara. I suppose you've heard by now that he kept female students around for sex? He'd leave Barbara sleeping in the tent and sneak over to the woman's shed. That's mostly why I never finished my degree: I got so disgusted with the whole thing. To answer your question, I thought Larry Todd was one of the most despicable people on earth. He got what he deserved and I now plan to marry Barbara."

Leaning back against the aging leather, Barry took a sip and continued, "I realize how suspicious that sounds and that's why I've asked you here. I want to eliminate any rumors before they even get started."

"Isn't Barbara Todd a bit older?"

"Eight years, not that it matters. Barbara and I share many interests. She's a horsewoman, you know. She said she'd love to ride our beaches sometime."

"Interesting. And how long have you and Barbara been planning to marry?"

"Our plans are just now crystalliz—"

"How long, Barry?"

"Actually, we haven't made any definite plans."

"Has Mrs. Todd actually agreed to marry you?"

"Barbara and I have always operated in the subtext—voice inflection, eye contact, you know how that goes."

"What'd she say, Barry?"

"When I said on the phone I hoped we'd be seeing more of each other now, she said, 'Well, that wouldn't be hard to arrange'—voice inflection, long silence, you know." He waved his pale hand through the air to explain the subtlety of it all.

"I see." Talbot stood. "Now I have a question for you. What were you doing Saturday?"

"Saturday I spent on the beach with a metal detector."

"At night?"

Barry stood, like his guest. "In the evening I went over to Friday Harbor for a movie, then—"

"Stop." Talbot took out a notepad and began writing. "I need the names of two people who saw you in Friday Harbor."

Barry stuttered at the abrupt question. "Margaret Boyer in the wine store and Nelson Thatcher at the visitors dock. Please don't th—"

"Stop." Talbot scribbled. "What did you do after the movie?"

"I came back here about midnight."

"Anybody see you?"

"No. But they probably heard the boat."

"Who's 'they'?"

"Woody, who brought you over. And perhaps the house-keeper."

"Woody said he worked for your father, where's he?"

"My father is on start-up at our anchovy cannery in Peru.

Woody's mistaken, he works for me. Are you sure you won't stay for dinner? Woody harvested mussels today.''

''No, thank you.'' Talbot finished his notes and walked to the terrace doors. ''We'll be getting in touch if we need you.''

Before Barry could say anything else, Talbot was across the lawn and down the stone stairs. The shepherds bounded behind, eager to play. Climbing aboard the *Jolly Roger*, Talbot raised the air horn over his head. Pressing hard on the plastic nozzle, he released two blasts of ungodly noise into the still afternoon air.

Next morning Laura and Terri sat in the gymnasium, rotating their kneecaps in tiny circles. ''Too bad you missed last night,'' Terri said, ''Norman gave back rubs.''

''My back's fine. What did he say about our knees?''

''Not much. Says all you can do is ice them or try to stretch out the upper thighs, your quads and stuff.''

Laura plucked at the long-sleeved jersey over her throbbing triceps. ''How'd the tournament go yesterday?'' If she kept Terri talking she wouldn't ask about Laura's own yesterday.

''Tandem fakes are taking over, even the college teams are doing it. And some of the shoot-out sets were unbelievable.''

''You do shoot-outs.''

''Not like some of these puppies. It's not even a fancy move for them, they learn it in camp. If you want to know the truth, when you get Rookie off her spiking kick, she teaches shoot-outs really well. She's the one who got my timing down.''

''I think people ought to leave Rookie alone. If spiking makes her happy, why not let her?''

''It's not that easy. Rookie got her scholarship on the basis of her setting. It's totally unrealistic of her to think she can change at this time in life. I personally think my parents have spoiled her rotten.''

Rookie bounced over. ''It's bimbo time. Tom Selleck's playing this morning and they're out in full force: Bimbos in the stands, bimbos in the aisles . . .''

"Stop trying to act so grown-up, Rookie."

"Stop trying to act so grown-up, Terri." The Watt sisters glared.

Laura broke in. "Rainbow Wahines for us this morning. How are we going to play this, same as Tuesday?"

"Five-one's working so far," said Terri. "My girls are comfortable with it."

Still sitting, Laura picked up a ball with her feet and tossed it to Rookie. "Come on, Rookie, help me warm up."

Out on the floor they joined the hundred-odd players rehearsing moves. Nikes chirped against the floor and volleyballs arched through the air like popping corn.

"I heard the Wahines are good," said Laura.

"We're taller than they are, I only saw one real leaper."

"Getting high isn't everything, Rookie."

"You say that because you can do it."

Flashbulbs began popping downcourt and TV floodlights went on. Rookie and Laura looked toward the dazzling brightness. "There he is."

A self-conscious, fortyish Tom Selleck, sporting a modified Mohawk and a bit too much tummy, walked out to take his place with the over-thirty males. Among volleyball players his six-four height made him only average. Ignoring the flashbulbs as much as possible, Selleck started stretching out his hamstrings, all the while making conversation with teammates.

"Poor guy, wish they'd leave him alone," said Laura.

"His hair is gross."

"He wears it up straight like that so he can go around incognito."

"Gross."

The whistle blew downcourt and they watched the Outrigger Canoe Club line up against Juggernaut Pacifica. Tom Selleck stood sheepishly in the lineup with his hands behind his back as the TV cameras rolled.

The Gatoraders whistle blew also, so Laura and Rookie joined the lineup and cased their own competition. With the exception of one lithe Caucasian, the Wahines were a troupe of compact Hawaiians in superb condition. When the pregame buzzer sounded, the Gatoraders gathered to hear Terri give the "short girl" talk: Spike 'em, spike 'em, and spike 'em.

Gatoraders had won the toss and elected to serve. Kimmy, starting out in service, floated an opening salvo into the Wahine backcourt. The Wahines returned it with a backspin requiring a bit more scramble than the Gatorader defense expected. They managed to move the ball up to Terri while Laura stepped outside for her spike.

"Laura."

"Yes." She leapt forward, faked left, and hacked the ball to the Wahine's midcourt floor. A nimble Wahine defenseman squatted into a stretched-out save and moved the ball to her setter with a controlled easy arc. The setter ignored the obviousness of the tall Caucasian—around whom the Gatorader block was forming—and passed to a leaping Wahine attacker who aimed at the taped-up fingers of Karen-Two blocking outside. The ball swept off her hand and the Wahines took over service.

On the next volley the Gatorade backcourt again moved the spinning ball to Terri, who this time telegraphed to Laura but back-set to Bushman. Bushman wiped it off the hasty block to the outside line but once again a Wahine defenseman moved up easily for the save.

Over and over Terri set up her spikers, trying all her stuff, both high and low. Laura and Bushman tried corners, off-speeds, and wipe-offs but the Hawaiian forecourt had perfectly mastered a soft block defense, while their spikers found the soft hands in K-Two's corner their favored target.

The serve passed back and forth eleven times and after eight minutes of play the score stood 5-5. Terri called a time-out and the Gatoraders slumped to rest.

Bushman wiped her face with a towel. "This pisses me off. It's like being eaten by a guppy."

Everyone looked to Terri. Her face was chalk white under the sweat and the circles around her eyes glistened blue-black. "We can take them, it's just going to take a while to find the hole."

Laura hated it when Terri looked this way, it always meant trouble. "If it's a matter of wearing people down, we'll go first, we're the heavies."

A roar rose up downcourt. The Gatoraders turned to the Outrigger Canoe game. They watched as the Outrigger setter tossed an arcing set at Selleck playing power left. Selleck spiked it cleanly to the floor and the fans exploded.

"Not bad, he just needs more court time," said Kimmy.

"Everybody needs more court time," grumbled Bush-man.

"Never mind Tom Selleck; what are we going to do about the Wahines?" asked Laura.

Terri sighed heavily. "Okay, let's keep the same rotation but I'm going to move up to work the block with Bushman. Is that okay, K-Two?"

"Great, my hand is killing me."

Rookie broke in, "I can block with Bushman." She could barely control her voice.

"I'm saving you for something else, Rookie."

"What?"

"Maybe backcourt."

"Oh no you don't. You said if I came here I could spike."

The whole team turned to the confrontation. Terri spoke directly into Rookie's eyes. "Rookie, Bush and I know how to firm up the block, and we need a good setter back there."

"You just want to spike yourself."

"Rookie," said Terri softly, "in college next fall Roberta's going to ask you to set, she already told me. It's too late for you to change positions."

"Terri, you can't keep bossing me around. I'm not the same as you."

"Rookie, look at me." Tears filled Rookie's eyes as she waited to hear the hard truth: "You can't spike. Five-feet-ten isn't big enough."

Rookie looked for a towel to cover her face. "I'm telling Mom." Bushman moved to put an arm around her but Rookie pulled away. Terri said, "Don't worry about it, Bush, she knows what she's gotta do." The time-out was over and the Gatoraders nervously took to the court, Rookie penciled in as setter.

It was Wahine side-out and they were dishing up wobbly spin serves to all comers. After fumbling the first one, Kimmy got under the second and popped it forward to the moving

Rookie, who barreled up the court out of nowhere. At first it looked as if she might not even lift her arms. But then at the last millisecond, just as they thought she would let it drop, Rookie shouted, "Up," to Laura and leapt into the air. Hanging midair six feet away, Rookie shot out the the ball horizontally at Laura, barely above net level. Laura shunted it over: The play was finished before the Wahines could bend their knees. From the stands Mrs. Watt shrieked with appreciation.

Laura beamed at Rookie. "Nice get."

Rookie smiled. She looked at Bushman to see if Bush wanted the next tip but Bushman shook her head to say "don't show your stuff."

With each point the offense became more and more wrapped around Rookie's off-the-wall setting. The hitters stayed on the balls of their feet, waiting to see what Rookie would do next. The defense found returning Wahine balls less and less the spinning threats they had been. At no time could anyone on the court determine how Rookie would next set up because she herself never knew until the last syncopated millisecond. Laura found it both exhausting and exciting. The Gatoraders built up the lead to 11–6, then after passing the serve back and forth for a while, took the game, 15–10.

For the second game the Wahines moved their formation back to guard their corners. The Gatoraders quickly found they could now keep the Wahines off-balance by working Laura's net game again. At 11–7 Bushman and Laura came out and K-Two and Lisa went in.

Laura hadn't talked to Bushman since leaving her at the mall Tuesday. They sat silently together on the sidelines, Bushman turning to watch a woman's game downcourt. Finally she broke the ice. "I thought you said UCLA wasn't any good."

"Are they here?"

"That's got to be them, the black girls playing for Westwood. They're eating that blue team alive."

They watched a leggy black girl—taller than Bushman and just as strong—walk a two-step up to the net and rivet a straight-down spike into the arms of the cowering blue defense. The rest of Westwood stood relaxed, in position, registering something between impatience and boredom.

"Find your letters yesterday?" Bushman asked.

"No."

"It was good you didn't stay with us after all. Dad called looking for you, and Mom was a little bent out of shape."

"What'd you dad want?"

"Didn't say, wanted to talk to you privately. That's the word that got Mom: 'privately.' "

"Are you mad at me too?"

"I don't know who I'm mad at. I guess you don't want to hang around me because you have a lot on your mind but I really wanted to tell you something the other day, just in case somebody else tells you first."

"What's that?"

"I went to bed with your boyfriend once. Before he was your boyfriend, though."

"Larry Todd? But you don't even like men."

"It was back before I really knew yet. It was after we came home from the Soviet tour and Mom had moved her stuff into the sewing room. I was really bummed out about it and Larry Todd was hanging around. He knew I was feeling crummy and beaded right in on me. It was a really dumb thing on my part, made me realize what gross-outs men really are."

"Bushman, I don't know what to say."

"Don't say anything. Game point here."

They watched Kimmy's overhead serve, the Wahine return, and their own back-row bump to Rookie. Rookie positioned a set for Karen, then lobbed a real one to Terri at right front, who swatted it into the crosscourt corner over the exhausted Wahine backcourt. The Gatoraders took the game, 15-9, and went back to the hotel for lunch.

Over a boisterous hamburger feed they decided the new offense was working so well they should continue it into the afternoon match. Rookie's high intensity was contagious. The Gatoraders floated 15-3 through their first afternoon game against the Checks-Techs on a winner's high. Everyone in the stands—including the TV cameras—came down to see what the excitement was, and by the middle of the game it was clear the Gatoraders would be five-second celebrities on TV news that night. They took the second game, 15–4, and went back to the hotel to celebrate in the Jacuzzi.

In the late afternoon, as Bushman slept in their room, Laura went down to the hotel lobby. Through the glass windows of the coffee shop she could see Rookie at the counter with an empty milkshake glass and several bags of candy.

Laura went in. "Rookie, hi. Could you order me a Coke, please? I need to make a phone call."

"It's easier up in the room."

"Bushman's asleep, and this is private."

"Oh." With unnecessary courtesy Rookie scooped her candy bags off the counter and moved to the far end.

Laura smiled appreciatively and punched Ho's number and her calling card number into the pay phone. Even if Ho did run with criminals, as Mr. Talbot maintained, he at least deserved an explanation for her leaving without a word.

"Ho Kauffmann speaking."

"Ho, it's me, I'm in Seattle. We won both matches today and we'll probably be on TV news tonight."

"My God, you're safe. Laura, the police have been here twice today. There's a Detective Talbot who's extremely unhappy right now. He says he's in the process of putting a summons out on you."

"Can you stall him?"

"Laura, stop it. I don't live farce and neither do you."

Laura looked at Rookie separating M&M's at the end of the counter. "Okay, Ho, here's the truth, I didn't really leave town. Tell him that. Tell him I'm in Bellingham at the museum and I've been cataloguing in the attic all day. There's no phone up there. If the police call back, that's all you need to say."

"Laura, this will not end well."

"Yes it will; don't worry."

She hung up and went down to Rookie, who was working her way through a pile of red M&M's, cracking them in half one at a time between her front teeth. Laura took a sip of Coke.

"Rookie, a friend in Bellingham is sick and I'm going up to see him. Want to play for me tomorrow?"

"Spiking? Sure."

"Don't tell your sister, okay? My knees are bothering me and you'd probably have to sub for me anyway."

"What's the deal with y'all's knees? Mine are fine."

Laura took a menu and started to write "B-E-L-L-I-N-G-H-A-M" on the back. "Don't worry about it, Rookie, you'll never be this old."

CHAPTER 7

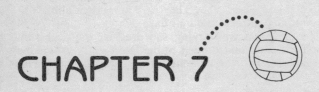

The last thing the museum janitor expected to see on his evening shift was the tall blonde girl who used to be a student intern. Darby hadn't seen her in a while and had heard she was in California. But here she was—tall as ever—tapping on the staff entrance to be let in. He opened the door.

"Hi, Darby, I'm Laura Ireland, remember me? I used to intern here."

" 'Course I remember, not many of them tall as you."

"Including the men. Darby, I left my rocks half-done and I have some free time now. Do you mind if I work late?" She brushed past him. "If I don't leave a better provenance on my rocks no one will ever let me in here again."

He swung the door closed using his little hop step to hide his gimpy leg. "All right, just call me when you want to leave so I can turn off the alarm."

"Thanks, Darby." Laura bolted up the grand Victorian

staircase to the second floor and, once there, took the tiny back stairs to the attic accession room. Under the huge hundred-year-old fir beams lay the castoffs of two cultures—Indian and white—oxidizing in acid-free boxes.

Laura made her way back through the shelves and found her white cardboard boxes exactly where she'd left them three years before. Her handwriting on the outside read, "Upper Skagit (Salish), Table rock site." She brought the boxes over to the accession table and found white paint and a labeling pen. From the boxes she picked out all the fishing sinkers—golf-ball-sized stones with indented waists—cleaned a spot with acetone, and brushed on a flash of white paint. She lined them up and counted: thirty. They made a perfect alibi; Talbot would think she'd worked all day.

While the paint was drying she dragged the accession ledger off the shelf and flipped to the latest entry. Someone had just accessioned the contents of an entire county farmhouse ending with #9200972.

"#9200973," she wrote, looking at the first sinker in the row. "Salish fishing sinker, basalt, 3.5 cm by 3 cm, circumscribed medial indentation, Skagit River." She blew on the black ink and saw ways to compress the notation. For the next one she wrote, #9200974, Fish snkr., basalt, 2.8 cm x 3 cm, circ. med. indentation, Skagit R." She worked her way down the row, shortening the description with each entry. She accessioned the basalt weights, then the chalcedonies, then the scoriac lavas.

When she had finished the entries she tested a white paint flash with her finger; it still wasn't dry enough to take the labeling ink. Very tired, she lay down across the chairs. The time was 12:08. Pulling up her sleeve, she examined the thin triceps scab with her fingertip. Why would someone shoot at her? It made no sense.

Maybe it had been the third person, the person who had drowned Adele Patterson. Did the scuba divers find the duffel bag down there? "Of course not," she said out loud. If Larry and Adele Patterson had been killed by some third person over Indian artifacts, he—or she—wouldn't have thrown them in the bay.

Laura looked up at the shelves of white boxes. "What's

the big deal? Who would kill for this stuff?" There was a mahogany mirror leaning against the shelves and to the woman upside down in the mirror she said, "Would you kill for this stuff?"

The blonde in the mirror had circles under her eyes, just like Terri's. There was nothing Laura could do about it, so she looked away. If Larry was killed because he was smuggling artifacts across the line, they were probably still out there somewhere, in his duffel.

So where was Larry's duffel?

He had had it with him in the phone booth, she remembered. She had heard the sound of its metal zipper through the receiver just before he began to read from her letters. Laura sat bolt upright: Then her letters were in his duffel; she was looking for it too!

Muffled footsteps sounded on the stairs. Laura dipped the pen in India ink and began writing the accession numbers on the sinkers. Darby found her hard at work. She looked up cheerfully at the gimpy-legged man. "Hi, Darby, are you going to clean the attic?"

"Just thought I'd see how you was doing."

"I've got to accession these, want to help?"

Darby chuckled. "I better let you do that. I'd like to close up soon, will you be long?"

"Actually I was hoping to work all night."

Darby's leathery windburned face struggled with this piece of information. "Something the matter?"

"I had a fight with my boyfriend and I can't go there."

"That so?"

"Yes. And I have to go back to Seattle tomorrow anyway, so I thought maybe I'd stay here for the night. If you let me."

Darby leaned against the shelves and slid his forearm into the bib of his pin-stripped overalls. Laura examined the shining red cheeks and amber eyes he protected with a squint—he had laid pipe in Alaska, she'd heard, even lost some toes to frostbite. Slowly he said, "You know, I usually don't cotton to people who won't give it to me straight." Laura felt his tough Alaska will mark up against hers. Like three tall blockers across the net.

"Oh," she said weakly.

"I know when something's wrong; I've been helping out students ever since they come. You wouldn't be here if you weren't in big trouble. What do you need? A telephone? Money? I can lend you some money."

"It's worse than that, Darby, and I don't think you can help. I wrote some letters to Larry Todd and now I can't find them. I might even get kicked out of school for it."

"Good Lord, you're not mixed up with that, are you?"

"Not like you mean. When I was his student I wrote him some love letters that I can't find up on campus. If his wife finds them I'll die. I just now realized they must be out at Adele Patterson's trailer."

"Well, go get 'em."

"I would, except a policeman told me they were watching the roads."

"Take a different road. Trailer's out on the Smith, isn't it?"

"Yes."

"Then that ain't no problem. Deputies'll be out on the Mt. Baker Highway in the Coffee Cup Cafe. I watched them once, saw them pick up a kid who stole a van. They never even moved. Kid drove by and they called down the road to have him picked up farther on."

"Is there a different way?"

"We can always find out." Darby nodded his shiny bald head to the map collection housed in a bleached hardwood cabinet in the corner.

Laura flashed an appreciative smile and darted over to the cabinet. Rolling open a wide flat drawer, she found maps and charts dating back to the 1850s. Most were land deeds and gold rush documents from settlement times. Closing the first drawer, she rolled out the next. The maps here were more recent; they started with Depression-era CCC maps of the Mt. Baker Forest. Walking her fingers through map corners, she found the fresh yellow and blue markings she was looking for.

"Here we are, a new topological map from the U.S. Geological Survey."

"Used these on the pipeline," Darby said.

Laura unfolded the topo map over her rocks and studied

the Mt. Baker Highway area. Geological Survey maps were so thorough that certain county farmhouses and barns were even marked. Maybe an isolated trailer off the Smith Road was too.

Laura found the pink-tinted Nammish Reservation and scanned down the Smith Road for something that could pass for the Patterson trailer. There it was, a red rectangular sliver at the end of a long dirt driveway. The high-tension power lines crossed nearby. And as she suspected, the trailer wasn't far from the Valley Highway as the crow flies, four miles overland to the north. Darby watched as she studied the terrain, folded the map, and put it away. The paint on the sinkers had dried, so Laura began painting on numbers. Darby left her deep in work.

It's difficult to sleep with somebody shaking your shoulder and Laura hated to be waked with shouting. "Honey, it's six A.M. You'd better go." It was Darby. "I get off my shift now."

Laura sat up and blinked at the row of fishing sinkers lined up before her. "Is it daylight yet?"

"Last time I looked."

Laura packed the sinkers and bounced down the stairs, almost pushing open the door. "The alarm," Darby called, and he hopped gamely down the steps turning one of his keys in the box by the door.

"Thanks, Darby. Don't tell anyone I was here, okay? I'd like to surprise them."

"You be careful," he said, avoiding her eyes.

Out on the street Laura inhaled morning air. She needed breakfast badly but didn't want to see Ho. He would be full of recriminations and all she needed was his army boots. Well, his army boots and his car.

Walking toward the business district, she looked for a restaurant that took credit cards. The Horseshoe Cafe had a Visa decal on the door. She went in and ordered the lumberjack's special, staying to drink coffee until 8:30 when Ho left for campus. She jogged to his apartment and let herself in.

The apartment was strangely silent; Chomsky didn't meet her at the door. Then she remembered that Ho sometimes left him on the fenced back porch during the day. Back in the bedroom she began outfitting for the woods. The apartment felt very strange without Chomsky low-riding at her ankles.

Ho was proud of his army days at Fort Lewis and kept his boots as a reminder. Happily, one of the first things she learned about Ho was that his size-eight foot was identical to her woman's nine and a half. Taking the boots from the closet and wool socks from the drawer, Laura sat on the bed. As she slid her foot into the left boot, her toes bumped into a foreign object. She pulled it out and held it to the light. It was a brown glass medicine vial with a quarter inch of powder in the bottom. Inside, the powder was white and fine, clinging to the sides of the glass. Almost bringing it to her nose, she realized what it was. White noise rushed in her head. She had never seen cocaine before.

So this is what Detective Talbot had meant about Ho. Spotting his Topsiders in the closet, she dropped the vial inside.

Lacing up the boots, Laura clomped to the kitchen and composed a careful note that asked only for permission to borrow the Honda. Strangely, even in the kitchen she could not hear Chomsky on the porch. She took Ho's car keys off the rack, then let herself out.

Hanging from the porch beam with a horribly long black tongue was Chomsky. Someone had looped his empty leash around the beam, then picked him up and attached him. He swung still warm in the soft breeze. Cocaine, Laura thought, with a curious detachment, and she stared at the swinging carcass, wondering if the perpetrator was spying on her this very moment. Looking past Chomsky, she walked across the gangplank to the alley.

Ten minutes later on the road to the trailer Laura was aware of a terrible pain in her hands. Looking down, she saw that her knuckles were as white as death as they gripped the steering wheel. She relaxed her hands and thought of Chomsky's swinging body; she took a deep breath.

Lake Whatcom, whose south shores she skirted, lapped at its tiny cove beaches. Out on the lake, sailboarders in wet suits rode the chilly breeze. As she turned onto the Valley Highway, snow-covered Mt. Baker appeared intermittently between the foothills. Komo Kulshan, the Indians had called Baker: the White Watcher. Laura could feel the soothing pull of its immense gravity as if it sensed her troubles. She took another deep breath.

By the time she reached Twelve Mile Grange she had banished Chomsky and the cocaine entirely. Her attention was totally occupied with counting the creek culverts crossing under the road. Beginning with big noisy Fish Trap Creek, she counted three culverts as she passed, then at the fourth, she turned onto a logging road and parked the car. From here on it was overland.

On the map Laura's hike looked pretty straightforward: two miles uphill following what the map called Green Creek, a quarter mile of ridge running, then a downhill turn to the power lines. But as Laura tramped up the hill she realized the map had overstated the case: The path up Green Creek was nothing more than a track for small animals. For anyone of human height the path was a swamp of devil's club and windfall branches, a minefield of rotten logs and slippery clay. She must have been the first upright animal to use the trail in years.

The woods up Green Creek smelled wet and green and reminded her of Larry. Even stumbling up the hill she couldn't help remembering happy summers at Keena when she and Larry took evening walks after digging. Sometimes they played an archaeology game they had invented, acting like the astounded Carter at Tut's tomb when they came upon anything out of the ordinary—trash heaps, gravel piles: "Why, Professor Ireland, notice the pyramidal style of this gravel pile: late mesolithic, I'd say." "Quite right, Professor Todd." She smiled at the memory.

Up high, the trail became so bad she walked in the empty creek bed, trodding on green velvet rocks that, weeks before, had cushioned early spring waterfalls. Most of the hardship of climbing was from ducking under, and scrambling over, fallen branches. By the time she had climbed high enough to see daylight over the top of the hill, Green Creek was nothing more than a moist gully. She followed the gully until it ended in a hollow. In the hollow she peeled back a mat of leaves in hope of finding springwater. There was none.

When the sun is shining, north in Whatcom County is the easiest direction to find. North is toward the Canadian Range, snow-covered and brilliant, with its toothy peaks named Lion's Gate, Golden Ears, the Sisters. Laura headed toward this range, brushing back branches and undergrowth at every step. She walked part of the way hunched over on a rabbit track, then came out to a deer trail which seemed like a boulevard in contrast. At the crest of the first ridge there was an outcropping with a view. She walked out to get her bearings.

To the north were the Canadians, to the east the glacial whiteness of Mt. Baker, and to the west the salt water and Vancouver Island. Million-dollar view in the middle of nowhere.

After the outcropping, the going became even rougher. Laura spent the next mile on a steep hillside flexing her feet and holding on with her hands. She lost her footing on loose rock and slipped on carpets of fir needles. At the crest of the next ridge she looked down and saw power lines crossing a clearing. Time to cut out downhill.

It was an incredible relief to walk with gravity. Laura dropped a thousand feet in ten minutes. When she arrived at the clearing near the power lines she found she was in a refuse dump: rusted oil drums and appliances from the sixties, the carcass of a Chevrolet propped on cinder blocks. Laura stepped carefully over a doorless refrigerator and the inner tank of a water heater. She silently invented a King Tut dialogue with Larry:

"I say, Professor Todd, we've stumbled on a late Caucasian ritual site."

"Quite so, Professor Ireland, see how the Chevrolet is facing the solstice."

Picking her way across the debris, she scanned the edges of the clearing for the way out. Had she missed the Patterson trailer entirely? It should be somewhere near the power lines, but she had lost her bearings. She walked tentatively down a dirt road through a sea of sword ferns, then after a mile stopped to turn back. Looking around, she suddenly spied the white siding of a trailer a few hundred yards ahead. She

walked as silently as possible to the site, then crouched behind salmonberry bushes to observe.

The trailer had certainly seen better days. Its roof was
carpeted with fir needles and small ferns grew in the gutters.
The skirting was gone in places, and in front of the kitchen
window a fifty-gallon oil tank sagged on a wooden frame.
Yellow police tape was draped over all the windows and there
were no cars in the clearing.

Laura walked around to the trailer front. The louvered
glass door was covered over many times with yellow tape.
POLICE LINE DO NOT CROSS, it said, over and over, in thick
black letters. To leave no doubt about what was expected, a
white cardboard sigh was posted on the jamb: KEEP OUT BY
ORDER OF WHATCOM SHERIFF'S DEPARTMENT. There was an
oversized padlock around the doorknob. Laura tried the knob,
found it locked, and withdrew her hand. Her fingers were
covered with pale gray fingerprint dust. She rubbed it off on
her pants.

Circling the trailer, Laura tried to peek in windows. At
the bedroom end of the trailer, clear plastic sheeting was
taped over the casement windows with silver duct tape. The
police tape had fallen off one of its nails and hung like an
old crepe paper streamer. Jagged shards of glass lay on the
ground and Laura could see more shards still attached in the
aluminum frames. Larry was shot in this bedroom, he must
have been standing in front of the windows. She peeled back
the duct tape at one corner and the plastic sheeting came with
it. Through the casement she unwound the tiny handle opening the window, then climbed up and over the threshold.

Inside, Laura's foot landed on something soft. Panic-
stricken, she clutched the window sash, waiting for her heart
to stop thudding, knowing she had stepped on something
dreadful. She refused to think of Chomsky. As her eyes adjusted to the dark, she saw she was simply standing on a bed.
Inked onto the naked king-size mattress was the outline of
the late Larry Todd. She climbed the rest of the way into the
room.

The room was covered with the fuzzy gray patina of de-
cay. Only the shattered windows above the bed signaled that
violence had occurred here. The brown stains on the mattress

and walls could have been from anything, she told herself. Fingerprint dust only added to the filthiness.

In the corner, a broken drawer was filled with dirty clothes. Two louvered closet doors, popped out of their sliding tracks, leaned against the wall. A pair of studded snow tires were propped in the corner.

Cautiously, Laura stepped to the floor. Somewhere in this mess had to be Larry's duffel. Inside, she was certain, would be her letters. She picked her way over to the bureau and opened the deep top drawer. It was crammed with bright nylon underclothes, most in terrible disrepair. There were panties with dead elastic, shortie negligees with cigarette burns in front, large-size brassieres too diaphanous to have done much holding up.

The next drawer was just as sorry. This one held overstretched knit pants, shiny floral shirts, and bright acrylic sweaters. Adele's favorite color had been purple. In the closet she found the most expensive garment in the room, a snow parka with a fox ruff meant for winters in Alaska. On the closet floor were wall-to-wall dead shoes. She walked into the hall and looked through the adjoining door into the filthiest bathroom she had seen since the toilets in Hong Kong.

The bathroom really wasn't as bad as the ones in Hong Kong because it didn't have that thousand-year-old smell. What it did have was a soft coating of human hair and dead skin, even in the bathtub. Under the film, on every shelf-sized space and in every cranny, were samples of all the grooming products available to Western man. There was hand cream, face cream, sample-size cold pills, broken compacts, eye pencils, lipsticks, hair spray, and enough over-the-counter medication to stock a small pharmacy. The toilet had no water in it and hadn't been cleaned since it left the Kohler plant twenty years before.

Laura looked for the duffel under the sink and in the linen cabinet. Finding nothing, she walked down the hall, dodging loose fiberboard panels with their toothy staples.

The second bedroom had cell-like proportions and was packed to the ceiling with fishing nets. Laura routed around underneath the nets and the bed. She broke two fingernails, but found no duffel.

The end of the hallway opened into the big room, a combined living and dining room with a kitchen at its far end. Laura stood trying to make sense of the chaos. Nowhere could she see the angle where floor met wall; all the peripheral space melded into a curve of late-twentieth-century junk. This wasn't the disorder of violence, it was the accumulation of years of random living. Stacks of magazines, newspapers, and corrugated boxes lined the walls. Tools and bric-a-brac lay on every flat surface.

After a moment, however, the everyday living space became apparent. It consisted of an empty armchair facing the TV. Next to the chair was a table and big ashtray, both covered with gray dust. Magazines were everywhere—*Prevention, Health, TV Guide*. The sofa was piled high with junk and two plaster cherubs hung upside down on the wall. Was that a joke?

Laura turned first to the living room furniture. The handles of the drum table doors were missing so she pried them open with her fingernails. Inside was a stack of newspapers, bags of clothes, and random pieces of kitchen plastic. She searched the cardboard boxes and all the shopping bags. There was no duffel in the big room. She moved on.

The kitchen had a dozen cabinets of dark-veneered oak. Opening cabinet doors one after another, she worked her way around the room. Under the sink was mouse bait and Drano, in a storage cupboard she found the water heater with a tiny carpet sweeper propped in front. One cabinet was full of home-canned jars of food, not only beans and fruit but also fleshy fillets of sacred salmon. The jars were dusty and untouched, their lids blooming rusty flowers. A cupboard by the stove was clearly the one most used. Inside were bright cans of Campbell's and Chef Boyardee. She must have been crazy to think her letters were here.

Closing the last cabinet, she looked at her filthy hands. If she didn't wash them they would leave fingerprints on the duct tape when she left. She was thirsty too, so she walked over to the kitchen sink and turned on the tap. Nothing happened. She waited for a sound in the pipes, heard nothing, then tried the hot water. Still there was no sound. In the sink a plastic dishpan was half-filled with water. Beside it was a yellow bucket: The trailer had no running water, Adele had carried it from a pump.

Laura closed the taps and went back to the bedroom. She knew Adele Patterson now: a woman who chain-smoked cigarettes and subscribed to *Prevention*, who canned Northwest bounty but ate Chef Boyardee. Climbing out the window, Laura smoothed back the duct tape. She picked up a fir branch and dabbed at the tread marks from her boots, then walked around the corner and stopped dead in her tracks.

Standing in the path was a short dark Nammish man who had been waiting for her. He didn't speak, but only stood blocking her escape.

Laura tried to smile. ''You must be Adele Patterson's husband.''

CHAPTER 8

Patterson stared at Laura for a moment, then said, "If you're looking for Adele she drowned in the bay."

"I know, a friend told me."

"You from the Fat Cat?"

"The college."

Patterson waited.

"I was looking for something of mine but it wasn't here," Laura said. "Are you going inside?"

"Me?" He took a step back as if knocked off-balance. "All I'm doing is waiting for the package store to open."

"Me too. I mean, I could use a drink too. Is there water around?" Laura pointed to a worn footpath.

"Not that way, that way's the toilet; pump's over here." Patterson walked briskly down the path as if happy to have a task. Laura fell in behind.

The shade in the woods was nearly black and under the

fir canopy gray-dead branches lay broken and rotting. Salal and fern brushed their ankles and the scented cold of the wet earth chilled Laura's skin. A hundred yards from the trailer Patterson stopped and squatted to examine a rusty hand pump on a concrete pad. Then he began pumping the handle vigorously, teasing up the air pressure. Laura put a hand under the icy stream and drank greedily from her cupped palm as Patterson watched.

"Water's real good out here," he said. "Only thing is, you have to pump by hand. Had an electric pump when the trailer was new, but it broke. They said eight hundred dollars for a new one. I said no way. Adele didn't care, said women always carried water, so what's it to her."

After drinking once more and wiping her mouth on her sleeve, Laura looked at Patterson and said, "Are you related to Macky Patterson?"

"My cousin. How do you know Macky?"

"I was a student at Western; he let me help with your genealogy project."

"I heard about you; you're the tall one. Is that how you know Adele?"

"I've never met Adele."

He looked at her oddly, taking in her clothes and boots. "You come through the woods?"

"Yes."

"You in trouble?"

Everyone seemed to be asking her that lately. "I was just trying to stay off the Mt. Baker Highway."

"Is this something to do with moving stuff over the line with Adele?" His eyes avoided hers, to show he had no right to pry into the actions of a white woman.

Laura shrugged.

"I thought so," he said. "Thought that might be how she got killed. She said she was gonna move something over for somebody—I told her not to."

"Did she really do it?"

"Don't know. She said she was gonna hide stuff in a load of furniture, tell 'em she was moving in with her sister across the line, then say they had a fight and move back. It's partway my furniture, so I told her not to, but I was in Alaska and couldn't stop her. Wouldn't have made no difference, I couldn't stop her anyway.''

"It must be hard on a family to work in Alaska.''

He nodded. ''Came out to Nammish to see our son but they said he's east of the mountains someplace. Police said I'm not supposed to sleep here tonight. I'm asking, how's that legal if this is my trailer?''

Laura shrugged. ''I don't know.''

"You heading back through the woods?''

"Yes, I'd better be going. Thanks for the drink.''

"Ah, that ain't a drink. Wait, not that way.'' He slapped his hand on his forehead. ''Jesus, now I see how you come. What'd you do, make your own trails?''

"Deer trails.''

"Jesus, honey, you be glad this ain't winter. You can't go back that way. Take the creek back.''

"Which one?''

"Smith Creek, over the rise. Follow it right on down to the Nooksack River. Creek's shallow in places and you can walk in the bed. Once you get to the river, there's big trails both sides, lots of people fishing. Nobody'll notice you there.''

"Thanks.''

"Well, good luck.''

"You too. And I'm sorry about Adele, she sounded like a really interesting lady.''

His dark face clouded with remembered pain. ''Yeah, she was full of beans.''

Two hours later Laura crossed Ho's kitchen porch. There was no trace of Chomsky. Not only had his carcass been taken down, but even his water dish and blanket were gone. Entering the kitchen, she saw the oddest assortment of people out in the dining room. Besides Ho, there was Detective Talbot from the police department and Dean Siecetti from the college. They watched silently as she stamped her boots on the mat. They were waiting for her to speak.

"No blisters, Ho, I used your wool socks.'' She sat on a kitchen stool, unlacing the boots. Ho did not reply. She crossed the dining room in her socks and kissed the top of his head. "I'm sorry about Chomsky."

"You saw him?" Behind his glasses his eyes welled with tears.

"It looked like he'd been hung up just before I got there."

"What time was that?" asked Talbot.

"Eight-thirty. Where is he, Ho?"

"The basement, in Mrs. Morse's freezer. I'm not sure what I want done with him yet."

She hugged him from behind. "I'm so sorry."

The Arts and Science dean, tired of waiting for his turn, leaned forward for their attention. "I don't mean to dismiss such a sad event so quickly but I have been waiting for nearly an hour to speak to you, Miss Ireland. Do you mind?" Siecetti was as elegantly turned-out as ever, wearing his familiar brown mohair jacket, this time over an ivory tattersall shirt and nubby brown tie. His hands he kept tidily on the table. "You had business out in the woods this morning?" he asked sweetly.

"No. I just took a walk, to clear my head. Mushrooms." She groped in her warm-up pocket and pulled out a handful of sodden matter. Placing it on her note to Ho she said, "Morels." The three men viewed the brown mess in silence.

Across the table the dean looked ready to slap her. Unlike Mr. Talbot, he was not used to being lied to and he worked hard to control himself. When he finally opened his mouth, he had mastered his rage and spoke with in a quiet foreign cadence. "I'm sorry you don't feel you can be more forthcoming with us, Miss Ireland. You must understand how difficult it is to believe you would go walking at a time like this."

"A time like what?" She hit him with her best blue-eyed innocence.

"I will continue, Miss Ireland. Although you are not forthcoming with us, I will be so with you. Since our last meeting I have done two things: checked on the information you asked for, and spoken with the authorities in Olympia. Concerning the first item, I am sorry to say that there is no information on this party one way or another, you must use your own discretion in this matter. For my part, if I were you, I would pursue the course you had plotted for yourself Wednesday—which is to say, go back to Seattle, but again, that is a matter for your discretion. Concerning the second item—speaking with the authorities in Olympia—I am happy to tell you that among ourselves we have determined a policy of proprietorship that might involve you soon, if it has not already.''

Laura nodded, not understanding a word he said.

Siecetti continued, ''You have indicated already that Dr. Todd might have been accumulating Indian artifacts during his term of employment with the state of Washington. I have been consulting with the attorney general and it is his considered opinion that anything accumulated by a state employee—as Todd was—rightfully belongs to the state. Therefore if you find—or have found—anything, you are to notify the university immediately. Is that understood?''

''Perfectly.''

''Good, then let me give you my card.'' He reached into his breast pocket. ''Perhaps you found something already this morning?''

''I went for a walk.''

''I understand your walk, but if these artifacts do turn up, they must be turned over to the state. The judicial system takes a very dim view of theft.'' He turned to Mr. Talbot. ''Isn't that right?''

''Dim, yes.''

''It is our job to help Detective Talbot find the tribe responsible for these two deaths and to expedite his investigations. Already he must have enough trouble, dealing with peoples so violent.''

Laura sat up straight. ''Violent? Compared to whom?''

''Excellent repartee, Miss Ireland.'' Siecetti looked at the gold wafer strapped to his wrist. ''In any case, I have stayed much too long enjoying Dr. Kauffmann's hospitality. I am here only to let you know if the artifacts come into your possession you will let us know immediately. Otherwise the attorney general will find it necessary to charge you with theft. I'm sorry to be so aggressive about this point but that is the manner in which it was presented to me.''

''I understand.''

"Well then, I must be going. Dr. Kauffmann, you have been a gracious host. I am truly sorry about your little dog." Siecetti smoothed the lapels of his coat and stood waiting for Ho to escort him to the kitchen door. As the two academics exchanged farewells at the door, Laura stared intently at the morels, avoiding Detective Talbot's gaze.

Talbot asked, "What time would you say you left here this morning?"

She looked up. "Nine."

"Is that when you saw the dog?"

"Yes."

"I found him at nine-fifteen, I must have just missed you."

"What were you doing here?" Laura asked.

Ho came back and answered, "Detective Talbot was patrolling our alley. When he found Chomsky he called me." He was about to sit down again but Talbot stopped him. "May I talk to Laura alone for a minute?"

"Certainly." Ho went into his office and closed the door.

The air crackled with tension. Talbot got up and paced to the window, looked down at the rose garden, then paced back. Glaring at Laura, he blurted, "At least we know your apartment manager saw you doing laundry Saturday night. At least we have that."

"You called Los Angeles?"

"Of course I called Los Angeles. It was either that or bring you in. I probably should have brought you in. Then we could have gotten to the bottom of this."

"You're really serious."

"Where *is* your brain? Two people have been killed, and now we've got hanging doggies. If anyone else turns up dead, it's my fault for not tracking faster. You better believe I'm serious."

Laura pushed back her chair and escaped to a corner of the room. "The dog's not related. I can't tell you how I know, but it's not. And if you want to ask me something, please use a normal voice, I don't allow anyone to yell at me." She crossed her arms and waited.

Talbot came over and stood very close. Unsure exactly what to do, he leaned his head against the paneling, making a small safe space between them. "Look, I'm sorry. I didn't mean to yell. I'm just having a real hard time buying all this. It's not looking squeaky-clean from my point of view."

She shrugged.

"Laura, listen to me, I can't give you any special breaks, but I'd like to be your friend. If you've done something wrong, you can help yourself out a whole lot by cooperating. The first thing you can do is tell me where you went this morning."

The space between them was warm and close. Laura breathed in the sweet air and looked at the hard curve of his pecs where she knew she could rest her head. She looked at the liquid kindness in his eyes.

"I can help," he said. He shifted his weight and Laura caught a glimpse of a holster strap under his sports coat; this was a policeman she was talking to, perhaps a very dangerous one.

"Don't get any closer."

"What?" He stepped back.

"And don't you dare use those big brown eyes on me."

He looked stunned.

"You think I don't know about you? I understand everything about you: Who you are, and how you work, and what's in it for you. You probably have a lot of luck batting those eyes at other women, but don't you dare pull that on me. I even know how you'd use me for your case: I'd go down and let you tape weepy stories about Larry Todd and me, and when it came time to go to court, you'd haul them out, drag me up here, then drop me. You don't care one fig leaf about me, or my reputation or anything. So that's how much I care about you, one hairy fig leaf."

Laura watched his face take the hit. She must have scored big because he looked away, almost turned to her again, then changed his mind and strode across the room. Peeling his portfolio off the table, he said without looking back, "Talk to you later," and then walked out the kitchen door.

Laura leaned against the wall, breathing hard. She listened to Talbot's shoes cross the landing and then heard Ho's office door squeak open. Ho peeked around the corner. "Is the coast clear?"

"Yes, come in."

"What happened out here?"

"He got close, I got mad."

Ho regarded her thoughtfully. "He's an attractive man, Laura."

"He's a policeman."

"He'd be a killer at cruising."

"He was cruising, and I resent it. Ho, none of this seems very important right now. Are you going to be all right?"

"I'd prefer not to talk about it, if you don't mind. I'll call Max when he gets out of class. Are you hungry?"

"Famished."

He led her back to the kitchen. "Did you know Theo Talbot is Creole, from Louisiana?"

"Theo," she said slowly, feeling the fricative with her tongue.

"He was so kind about Chomsky. Had him cut down and wrapped in his blanket when I got here. He really is a most attractive man, and I don't mean just physically." Ho moved around the kitchen, collecting sandwich things.

"I don't much care about him right now, and since all your company's left I have something important to say to you. What I learned about you this morning was so shocking it nearly tore my insides out. If Chomsky hadn't been so dear I'd almost say you deserved what you got."

Ho sat down heavily. "Whatever are you talking about? You've never cared about my life-style before."

"I'm not talking sex preference, I'm talking about your cocaine. I know what's going to happen to you, Ho. The girl upstairs from me was doing it and she tried to steal my computer monitor."

"Laura, I don't snort."

"Please don't lie to me, I found your stash."

"Where?"

She picked up an army boot and jiggled it in front of him. "I put it in your Topsiders."

Ho pivoted and left the kitchen. She heard him walk first to the bedroom, then the bathroom. The toilet flushed and he came back holding up the empty brown vial.

Laura said, "You mean the cocaine wasn't yours?"

"My holiday party was busted this year. There didn't seem to be any reason to tell you, and I'm certainly not proud of the fact. It made the *Tribune*, caused a terrible stink. A pitiful little boy who used to hang about the edges of our crowd was dealing and doing cocaine heavily. He, of all people, turned informant. Incredible vermin. He named names, told when the Canadians would come, awful things. I don't know whose vial this is, but it must have been there since December." He pitched it in the trash and said, "Will roast beef be all right?"

"Roast beef will be wonderful."

Ho cut thick slices of wheat bread and spread them with Dijon and mayonnaise. "You should hear Theo Talbot talk about food. He says he makes his own mayonnaise, 'my-nez' he calls it. I think he's quite a nice boy, what do you think?"

"I don't have an opinion. Did he ask about me?"

"Extensively. Asked about your background, whether you'd been in trouble before . . ."

"What did you say?"

"I told him about your speeding ticket."

"You did not." Laura sliced Swiss cheese to move things along.

"I told him that you probably haven't had much time to get in trouble considering how committed you are to your studies."

"What did he say then?"

Ho turned to look at her. "You really have it bad, don't you?"

"I do not. And I know how to protect myself."

"That may well be, but I find conversations in which one person is unaware highly unsatisfactory. If you can't confide in me about Theo Talbot, then at least tell me why you're taking such pains over your old love letters. I think I've held my peace admirably up to this point, but I am beginning to feel quite put upon."

"Don't worry about me. You've got your own problems with Chomsky."

"And that's why I want you to know I won't be this accommodating indefinitely."

Laura put down the cheese slicer and put her arms around the little man. "Ho, I'm in so much trouble."

"Yes, I thought so. You must remember how well I know you. Here, sit down and eat." Ho poured Laura a glass of milk and opened a beer for himself. He took the first draft and pondered the ceiling. He said, "In England there's a beer called Courage; I think of that sometimes." He took another sip.

"Very well," he said, "let me start your story for you. You wrote love letters to Larry Todd and you came back here to get them. They weren't in his office and they weren't out in the woods—I assume you went out to the Smith Road place?"

"Yes."

"And for some reason you can't leave well enough alone?"

"They weren't just love letters, Ho. I helped Larry steal artifacts and I wrote about it in the letters."

"Oh, Laura."

"I didn't do it intentionally, and I stopped as soon as I saw what was happening to me."

"Or more correctly, when you saw what you were doing."

"Yes, that's what I meant."

"And you think something"—he considered the word—"*untoward* might happen if the letters surface?"

"If someone gives them to Barbara Todd. She hates me, she could wreck my career. Or if, as Siecetti says, the state of Washington gets the artifacts and Larry's duffel bag—where I'm almost positive my letters are—everything will sit in an archive for twenty years until some research student comes along and reads about how these old geezers back in the nineties stole things from the Kwakiutls. Can you imagine?"

Ho sipped beer. "So what do you need from me?"

"I've got it figured out. There's almost no chance my letters are at Larry's house because he never went there. So if they aren't in his office or Adele Patterson's trailer, the only other place they could be is in the storage sheds at Keena."

"You want to go to Keena Inlet?"

"You said Max Eberhardt has a boat. It's Friday and we can tell him we want to go on a weekend jaunt."

"Oh, Laura."

"Please stop saying that, I feel bad enough already."

"As you should. What I feel bad about is that you didn't confide in me three years ago when these problems started."

"They weren't problems then."

Ho finished his beer and stood. "I was going to call Max anyway. We can see if he's up for a trip."

Laura cleared the dishes and bundled up the garbage to take it out. Back in the alley she raised the heavy dumpster lid and, glancing through the space between the lid and the dumpster, saw a shadowy figure in the parking garage across the way. As she put the lid down, the figure quickly slipped back into the dark basement. Laura closed the dumpster and went back inside.

Ho came into the kitchen. "Max said he'd be delighted."

"There's a policeman watching us from the parking garage."

Pushing back the curtain, Ho looked out. "Those people really go too far," he said. "Is it Theo Talbot?"

"No, I would have recognized Talbot. It must be one of his flunkies. Do you think they know about the cocaine?"

"That business is over and done with. I've half a mind to call the ACLU."

"Not now, we need to go to Keena."

"Well, I'll be hanged before I allow the police to follow us."

Laura looked out over his shoulder. "So what do we do?"

"I don't know. But I know what Max would do."

"What?"

Ho ignored the question and rubbed his hands together in anticipation. "What's more," he continued, "perhaps we can enhance the ruse by enlisting Alida Morse. Oh my. This is going to be fun."

"Ho, what are you talking about?"

With a gleam in his eye he said, "I'll show you what hanging around with theater people does to you. First of all, could you please call a taxi and tell them we need a ride to the marina in one hour—that's when Max expects us. I will go downstairs and see if we can persuade Mrs. Morse to lend her monumental resources to our endeavor.''

An hour later Mrs. Alida Blanche Endicott Morse stood on the front porch of Endicott House smiling at the yellow taxi on the street. Her corgis tugged on leashes, eager for adventure. Mrs. Morse adjusted the beady-eyed dead minks around her neck and called back over her shoulder, ''The taxi's here.''

''We're coming,'' called Ho. ''I'm a bit slow in these high heels.''

''Take them off.''

''I need the practice for outside.''

The taxi honked and the gaggle of people and dogs spilled down the steps of Endicott House. First came Mrs. Morse with two corgis on leashes. She turned to talk with a lanky blond man in a tight tweed jacket carrying a leather book satchel. Clambering slowly behind was a short dark woman in an ankle-length ivory suit, having trouble with her heels. The group chatted cheerily all the way down the steps to the street. They quit the charade only when they were safe inside the taxi.

Mrs. Morse chose a backseat corner, arranging one corgi in her lap and the other on the floor. To Mrs. Donahue clipping flowers across the street she nodded her elegant blue head; poor Mrs. Donahue never had such exciting times with young people. Turning to ivory-suited Ho beside her, Mrs. Morse said, ''If you want me to ride around for a while after you've been dropped off, you must leave some money. I don't mind ruses but I do mind paying for them.''

Fighting the constraints of his silk suit, Ho leaned forward to Laura in the front seat. She was dressed in Ho's tweed jacket and her long hair was tucked into a motoring hat. For trousers she wore his corduroy pants. These she covered to the knee with ribbed wool socks giving the effect of her having on plus fours. On her feet were black wing tips.

''Laura, give Mrs. Morse a twenty from my wallet, will you?'' Ho glanced at the incredulous taxi driver and improvised, ''Why do you suppose Max decided to give a dress-up party on his boat? After all, it's still the middle of the day.''

"Beats me, Ho, he's your friend.''

"He's so eccentric.'' Ho slipped off Laura's heels and straightened the pencil-thin skirt around his legs. The skirt was so long that he had needed to shave only the bottom few inches of his legs. For that he was thankful.

Mrs. Morse repositioned her feet around the corgi's tail and regarded Ho thoughtfully. "Tuck in your blouse, dear. And I do want my wig back, you understand? I wear it to the hairdresser's on occasion. Now, tell me, what am I to say when the cops come around?''

The driver's ears pricked up and Ho stammered, "Tell them the party has been moved out to the islands and we no longer need them to direct traffic.''

Mrs. Morse saw her mistake and covered quickly. "I do hope you win the prize at the party this time, your costumes are *much* better than last years'.''

"Yes, we were terrible last year,'' said Ho.

"Tell me again what you went as?''

Ho glared. "Romans. Nero and Aggripina.''

"So old-fashioned,'' murmured Mrs. Morse. She scratched the corgi's head and smiled out the window at Bellingham.

CHAPTER 9

"You certainly don't look like boatsmen."

Max Eberhardt was disgusted. Always dressed impeccably himself—today in an Aran sweater and Greek sailor's cap—he insisted that people who boated with him abide by the unwritten rules of yachtmanship. As he watched the high-heeled Ho limp ridiculously down the dock, he glanced at his spotless white pants and stroked his sculpted Vandyke; one always wanted to be sure he himself was not the offender.

Ho Kauffmann enjoyed provoking Max. Mimicking a bag woman's shuffle, he held up his shoe bag and said, "It's all right, dearie, my Topsiders are in my purse."

Max ignored his friend and extended a hand to Laura. "Come aboard. I'm Max Eberhardt. So glad to meet you."

Ho was the one who really needed a hand. Laura's ivory silk skirt was so tight around his legs he couldn't step over to the boat. He studied the problem for a moment, then un-zipped the skirt and climbed aboard in his panty hose.

"Blast, man," Max snapped, "you're right in front of the yacht club."

"Sorry."

"Just cast off."

Ho headed for the bow to work the lines.

"Damn it, Kauffmann, get off the foredeck. Go down and put on some clothes." Max went forward to cast off, then climbed to the flying bridge to pilot the sleek twin-engine inboard out toward the mouth of the bay.

Laura followed Ho to the cabin, changed clothes, and made instant coffee for Max. Balancing coffee in one hand, she made it up the ladder and through the vinyl door of the flying bridge without spilling a drop.

Max sat in one of the cushy swivel armchairs, steering the boat with two fingers. He looked up. "Laura, how nice. Since you're up here, could you look in the console for our charts? I have them for everything north of Seattle but we never use any of them."

Laura sat down and rummaged through the console. "Why not?"

"Ho is still quite green, hasn't any sea legs. Rarely do we venture past the close islands."

"Here's what we want, 'Canadian Hydrographic Service: Nanaimo to Sonora Island.' " Laura spread it out on the console.

Ho came up and found Laura and Max studying the chart. He studied too, only finding his bearings after he realized that Bellingham was not on the map at all, but was much farther south. "Has anyone ever counted all the islands?" he asked.

"They try sometimes." Laura watched Ho fight to keep his balance on the moving deck. "People like to say there are between four hundred and seven hundred—depending on what you count—but only a hundred and fifty are named—depending on who you ask."

"So how do we get to your beloved Keena?"

Laura dragged a finger up the blue Straits of Georgia separating Vancouver Island from the mainland. "Up the straits for a few hours to a gas stop at Albert Bay. Then we make a shorter run back across to the mainland and into Keena Inlet. The Tsamian Reserve is in that cove, there.'' She pointed to a bulge in one of the blue-tinted waterways snaking into the coastline.

''Why isn't it marked on the map?''

''The Tsamians got it taken off about ten years ago. They didn't like boaters coming in asking for gas and hamburgers.''

''You could make a killing on hamburgers in a spot like that.''

''Ho, this is going to be a really different place, okay?''

''I understand that.''

''Just be heads-up about what's going on.''

Max broke in. ''Before we go motoring so grandly up the straits, we need to present ourselves to Canadian customs in Bedwell Harbor. They take a dim view of unannounced American boats.''

Max piloted them out past the final mottling of American islands—Sucia, Matia—and into the Canadian ones. And after he had guided them into Bedwell Harbor to declare his half bottle of scotch at customs, he swung out again into the dazzling brightness of the straits for two hours of open running.

Ho quickly bored of the sunlit splendor and went down to the cabin with a copy of *Tristram Shandy*. After a while Max turned to Laura. ''What's the possibility of buying some craftwork in Keena?''

Laura shifted in her armchair. ''I don't know. What did you have in mind?''

''I'm a collector, I'm interested in the beautiful.''

''Do you have a lot already?''

''A bit. My finest piece is a Bella Coola ceremonial mask. I was hoping to acquire a blanket or weaving for the stairwell, and maybe add to my Argolite collection. But I would seize upon anything of beauty.''

''Who do you buy from?''

He turned to look at her. ''I pick up things here and there.''

Laura pulled up her knees and pretended to fall asleep in

the swivel armchair. With the warm sun and engine drone, sleep was not hard to feign. After a time Max throttled down; Laura jerked up and Ho came up from the cabin.

"Is something wrong?" Ho asked.

"It's Albert Bay, our gas stop."

Ho eyed the sweep of houses and shops facing a single mile-long street that ran the curve of a huge bay. "This is a big town."

"Biggest in the area," Laura told him. "Home of the Timpkish."

"I thought you called these people Kwakiutl."

"Timpkish is one of the bands in the Kwakiutl language group. They're one of the biggest bands and are known as the best fishermen. Actually the whole Kwakiutl thing is sort of a bad joke."

"What do you mean?"

"Around the turn of the century the anthropologist Franz Boas labeled about a dozen bands 'Kwakiutl' because they all shared the same language. Except in this case the bands had never considered themselves united, they hadn't even been each other's 'other.' And to make matters worse, Boas didn't even get the name of the language right. It's Kwakwala, not Kwakiutl. Anyway, it's been eighty, ninety years and the literature calls them all Kwakiutl, so they're used to it. And it's easier when talking to whites."

"You're calling them 'bands,' " said Max.

"Canadian bands, American tribes."

"My God." Ho jerked forward. "Is there a carnival in town?"

Laura grinned and handed him the binoculars. "No, take these, you'll be surprised. Scan for the white clapboard church. What you're looking for is next to that."

Max grew curious. "What's he found?"

"I'll let Ho tell you."

Ho squinted through the glasses. "I would say I am looking at a cemetery. But it's the most extraordinary cemetery I've ever seen, almost like a circus midway. There are colored posts and markers—red, black, white. I see killer whales, dolphins, some crosses. Is it Christian?"

"Methodist."

"Then why is there an arch with killer whales on it?"

"That's not even the best one. Look for the raven memorial in the far corner."

"Yes, I see it. Extraordinary."

"That's the Tsamian corner; they're considered the best artists. They come over here to bury their dead."

Ho looked for a minute more. "Astounding. And the missionaries let that sort of thing go on?"

"You don't tell someone how to grieve for the dead."

Max said, "Perhaps we can have a closer look later but right now there is a more urgent task at hand. Where do I tie up, Laura?"

"Visitors dock, far east end."

"Can we eat here? I haven't had a proper meal since breakfast."

"Certainly. The Blackbird Cafe is by the docks."

Max dropped the boat down to low gear and Ho recognized the signal to put out the docking bumpers and scrambled to help. On the commercial docks, dark Timpkish men looked up from their net mending to examine the Chris-Craft's markings. On the visitors dock there was another man, taller than the others and not in work clothes. He carried a legal satchel and stood alertly watching their boat.

Laura went down to the bow and tied on a line to jump off with at landing. As they puttered into the dock, she looked up at the tall man's face. She was stunned to see Theo Talbot. He stared back so fiercely that Laura looked away and smoothed the bowline.

The boat inched up to the dock and Laura leapt off in front of Talbot. Max cut the engines, leaving a deafening silence. There was nothing to do but speak.

Laura tried her power smile. "Mr. Talbot. What a surprise."

His mouth was stiff with anger. "You can't stay put, can you?"

"Just off for the weekend. How did you get here?"

"Island Air. I'm waiting for the mail boat over to Keena."

"But it's Friday afternoon; the mail boat won't come again until tomorrow."

"Missed it by thirty minutes."

Ho stepped forward. "What a coincidence. We're going to Keena too, why not come with us?"

"That would really help, if you don't mind."

"Not at all." Ho called over his shoulder. "Max, we've picked up another passenger." Max climbed down from the bridge.

Ho continued, "This is Theo Talbot from the police department."

Max's voice was cold enough to freeze penguins. "Mr. Talbot and I have met."

"But, Max, you don't understand. He's the Creole cook I was telling you about."

Laura gathered the docking line in lazy loops, wondering at the ugly air between Max and Talbot. What had Max done? Maybe his penchant for collecting Indian art was more important than she knew. Had Max known Larry Todd? Laura's curiosity was piqued; clearly it was time to chat up the detective. Cheerily she said to Talbot, "We were going to get something to eat. Would you like to join us?"

Max made a noise deep in his throat.

"I've already eaten, thank you," said Theo. "I can recommend the Blackbird."

"Then perhaps you'll keep us company," she urged.

Max gave her a look that could kill.

Dropping back to walk with Theo, she hit him with a blast of orthodontic perfection. "It's good you like the Blackbird because it's the only restaurant in forty miles."

"Don't bother turning it on, lady. I'm mad enough to spit teeth."

"What are you going to do—arrest me?"

"I just might if we were home."

"You can't up here?"

"Here I call a mountie, just like you."

Max stood on the boat, unwilling to disembark. "Ho, I think I'll fix myself something here. You all go ahead."

"Max! You were the one who was so hungry."

Laura looked to Ho for explanation but Ho only shrugged. Climbing aboard the boat, she grabbed Max by the hand and hopped back over to the dock dragging him with her. Up the wooden dockside stairs she physically led him by the hand.

He walked stiff-legged like a recalcitrant child. Talbot looked back continually, not knowing whether or not to bow out of the group. To cover the awkwardness of it all Ho read the restaurant sign: BLACKBIRD CAFE: GOOD FOOD. I've always like that description: 'good food.' It's 'cuisine' I don't trust.''

"I never eat cuisine," said Theo.

"Even in Louisiana?"

"Especially in Louisiana."

Laura broke in. "Well, don't worry, the closest cuisine is in Vancouver and there are forty miles of fir trees between us and it."

Inside, the restaurant smelled of frying grease. The customers were all black-eyed Kwakiutl in one of two varieties: single men in baseball hats at the counter and young women with toddlers in the booths. A tiny girl with gleaming black eyes stood in a booth clutching a french fry. She stared at Laura's blonde head as Laura walked across the room. Everyone else did the same.

The four Americans sat at a corner table and a dark heavy teenage girl came over. The restaurant went silent to hear what the outsiders would say.

Laura smiled. "Coffee, please."

The waitress brushed back her crow-black hair and went to the kitchen. The owner, a middle-aged man, peered out.

Their meal was Northwest short-order: fried oysters, clams, potatoes, and a side of coleslaw. There was tartar sauce and malt vinegar for the fries, and good coffee. When they finished, the owner peeked around the corner once more and came over with the coffeepot. They owed him—and the rest of town—an explanation.

Knowing the etiquette, Laura took the lead. "You're one of the Hunts, aren't you? I remember you from when I worked over in Keena on the archaeology project."

The Indian nodded his head. His taunt brown skin stretched like a drying hide over his high Timpkish cheekbones. "Robert Hunt," he said. "My cousin's the other Robert Hunt, the one who chains himself to trees."

"Then you're from a famous family."

"We kind of think that one's a little touched in the head."

"But don't you agree with him? I don't think they should clear-cut forests either."

"Can't run a business chained to a tree. I remember you. You used to come through here with that professor from Washington."

"Larry Todd."

"Haven't seen him in a while." Robert Hunt looked out the window and scanned the bay as if looking for Todd's boat. "They finished working in Keena?"

"Larry certainly is. He got killed last weekend."

"Jeez." Robert Hunt looked around, he needed a chair to sit down. "Jeez. I didn't know things got that rough down in Washington. He was real important, wasn't he?"

"Some people thought so."

"I'm surprised they killed him. Guess they had to do something, making so much trouble. They shouldn'ta killed him though."

Theo broke in. "They?"

"Oh, I don't know who killed him or nothing. I just thought you meant it was somebody who didn't like him stirring things up like that."

"I don't understand."

Hunt waved the question away with his hand. It was indiscreet to ramble on and he had talked too much already. He looked to Laura for help.

"It's okay, Mr. Hunt. Mr. Talbot's a policeman and he needs to know all this anyway."

Hunt looked around the room at his silent customers for approval, then motioned for the waitress to come take the coffeepot. He put his hands on his knees, then began: "See, Tsamian's been trying to break off from the rest of the bands, First Nations they call it, real serious these days."

"Now Tsamians are only the people over in Keena?"

"Yes." Hunt relaxed under the easy question. "They've always acted real proud over there, like they're better than everybody else. Real strict with their kids. You go over there and there's nothing to do. They always keep to themselves, say they're separate."

Theo shrugged and fiddled with his spoon. "So what's wrong with that?"

Hunt leaned forward, using his short muscled arms for support. "No, you don't understand. All the bands are real mixed in, married back and forth from way back. Right now Tsamian's considered just a little part of Timpkish, four, maybe five big families. They need things over here in Albert Bay, but when they come over they're so stuck up they won't barely talk to you. But, boy, they sure are happy to come over and use the hospital and co-op."

"The co-op's for fish?" Theo asked.

Hunt's look said Theo was an idiot child. "That's what a co-op is: a fish cannery. Fishermen own it, run it."

Theo nodded. "Then why are they breaking off from the Timpkish?"

"Tsamians want their own identity, you know? Also they get their old fishing grounds back, the whole river. They've been getting the university people to do their dirty work for them but I don't think they'll really bring it off. They're crazy if they think the government is going to give them the whole Keena River, all that timber and fishing. And then, when you're finished breaking off, you're not even known as Kwakiutl anymore." He gestured south. "On the outside everybody knows Kwakiutl, good as Haida. But have you ever heard of Tsamian?"

To keep things amiable, Talbot said, "But look at it from the Tsamian side: all that good fishing. You'd go for it too if you lived there."

"No. I tell you why they're doing it—they're doing it to cause trouble. Some people even think they're the ones stole our museum stuff, they think it's theirs."

"When did that happen?"

"Last fall. After that, we just boarded up the windows until we can fix the security."

"Security was bad?"

"Yeah, things were just laying out, we trusted everybody. Somebody came in and took all the best things—silver, knives, the Dolphin Ladle, a real famous copper shield." Hunt looked at the dark faces around the room, searching for shared indignation.

"What day last fall?" asked Theo.

"November. Maybe we lost some before that, too, but

we don't know because we didn't have the inventory. But in November someone stole things flat out. They sell them in New York for high prices.''

"You found them in New York?"

"No. No. Kwakiutl sells big in New York all the time, see what I'm saying? Maybe they'll find ours in New York."

"Who do you think stole them?"

Hunt shrugged vaguely. "A dealer or somebody. We've been watching and they didn't show up on the market yet. Police are even checking London, England. Way back, Captain Vancouver took some Kwakiutl stuff there. It's still there, in the museum.''

"That so?"

"Old Dinky—he's dead—he's seen it." He called to the waitress, "Sherry, what's that museum in England where the Kwakiutl is?"

"British Museum."

Max choked on his coffee.

"That's right." Robert Hunt nodded. "The British Museum, and the German Museum. There's more Kwakiutl in the German Museum." He turned to Theo. "When did you say that professor was killed?"

"Early Saturday evening."

"Then that makes sense about how they was acting." Hunt looked coyly out the plate-glass window. "But I don't want to start something.''

Theo pursued. "It makes sense about how *who* was acting?"

Hunt only stared at the bay, chin raised in silent eloquence. Laura's eyes told Theo to try again.

"Is there something you should tell me, Mr. Hunt?"

"Maybe," said Hunt. "But I don't want to start something with the Tsamians."

"You won't be starting anything. What did they do?"

"Well, real early Sunday morning they come into the float here, say they had engine trouble. Everybody else had come back from fishing Saturday."

"They have any fish?"

"A little bit. But everybody else did real well."

"What season are they fishing?"

"Halibut. And you know the other strange thing about it on Sunday?"

"What's that?"

"They were letting that woman drive the boat."

From the steps of the Blackbird, Max scanned for the weather pole. While they were eating the sky had turned pewter gray, and as they climbed on the Chris-Craft, wet ragged circles began to form on the fiberglass deck. Ho went below again with *Tristram Shandy* and Laura followed Max up to the flying bridge. Theo hesitated, then ducked into the cabin with Ho.

Out on the straits the rain began in earnest. Max turned on the wipers and began matching up the islands on the chart with the islands outside his windshield. Laura watched how efficiently he navigated from charts.

"Where'd you learn piloting, Max?"

"Entirely self-taught."

"You're following the exact route of the Keena mail boat."

"Nothing special in that. The course through the islands is self-evident if you look at the charts."

"I'm going below, want anything?"

"No, thank you, I'm very comfortable. And when you're down there, remember: Whatever your young man tells you about me, it's all a matter of perception."

Laura flushed. "He's not my young man."

Down in the cabin she found both Ho and Theo stretched out comfortably on plaid bolsters. Theo was organizing papers from his satchel. He looked perfectly at home with his papers and reminded Laura of an office worker or scholar. From over the top of his folders he gave her an appraising look.

Ho looked up from reading just in time to catch the look between Theo and Laura. He closed his book and roused himself from the bolsters. "Shouldn't leave Max up there alone, I'll go keep him company." He slid back the cabin door. "Ugh, still raining. Laura, how much longer?"

"Another hour. Close the door."

The door banged shut and suddenly Laura and Theo were

alone in the snug little room. Laura took out one of the paperbacks from the shelf and flopped down where Ho had been. Opening the book near the middle, she stared at the black typeface. Theo watched her a moment, then returned to his work. After a time of peeking over the top of her book, she finally broke the silence.

"You said you went to graduate school."

"Off and on."

"Social work?"

"Too complicated to explain."

"That's what you tell people you don't want to talk to."

"Is it?" He looked at her and then down at his papers again.

"What happened between you and Max?"

"I'm afraid that's privileged information."

"Is it something I should know about?"

"No."

"Is it something about Larry Todd?"

"I said it's privileged. I couldn't tell you if I wanted to."

"But I know something about Max that might be important: He buys Indian artifacts and he's piloting us through the islands exactly the way the regulars do. I think he's been here before."

"I'll make a note of that."

"You don't understand. I want to help you now."

"Did you leave travel plans at the police station? That would have helped."

"No."

"You've put me in an awkward situation, wouldn't you say?"

"I guess."

"And I don't for a second assume that you and these two nonboaters are out for a weekend cruise up the coast."

"Max is good; it's Ho who doesn't know beans from ballast."

"What are you doing out here anyway?"

"Looking for something."

"Your love letters."

"Yes."

"I'm surprised you didn't try the trailer."

"I did try the trailer."

She watched his nostrils flare and quickly lied, "But I just went in and out. I was too afraid to stay."

Theo looked at her a moment, then rumpled his hair. "So what do we have now? Two counts of trespass and failure to report whereabouts. I wish I weren't here."

"I wish you wouldn't talk like that, I know I can help."

"How?"

"I can tell you somebody who probably didn't kill Larry and Adele Patterson."

"Who's that?"

"Adele's ex-husband. I don't think he even knew Larry, and he really seemed to love Adele."

"How do you know Patterson?"

"I met him at the trailer."

"Damn it. We told him to stay away."

"It's his house, where do you expect him to go?"

"Anyplace he wants but a crime scene. Please stay away from Patterson. The only thing we know about him right now is he wasn't on his cannery shift Saturday in Dutch Harbor, Alaska."

"He wasn't?"

Theo didn't answer and looked again at his papers. After a minute Laura said, "I didn't tell you I was leaving town because you were having me watched; you already knew what I was doing."

"Me?"

"It wasn't you personally, it was one of your other minions."

"When?"

"This morning."

"What did he look like?"

"I don't know. He stayed in the shadows in a garage."

Theo studied her. "Laura, I swear to you no one from the department was tailing you. Not to my knowledge anyway, and I'm pretty sure I'm still in the ball game. If anyone actually was tailing you, that person is probably dangerous, or may think you know something that endangers him. I wish I could make you see how serious this is."

Above their heads they heard Max gear down, then pound

on the floor as a signal. Laura and Theo went up to see what was wrong.

Outside the rain had let up. All around them green forested mountains jutted straight up like skyscrapers. Down the mountainsides, slow-motion waterfalls fell in silent cascades. The salty chop of the open water had given way to green rolling swells. Above them a hawk rode motionless in the updraft. Max shifted to neutral, and for the first time seemed disoriented. "Unless the inlet is that cleft ahead we've missed it entirely."

Laura said, "You've done exactly right, Max; the cleft is wider than it looks. When we round this point, you won't believe your eyes."

As they motored around the last green sugarloaf, the rough salt seas became glassy and serene. The boat stopped pitching and they slipped into the entrance of Keena Inlet, a deep cold channel cut in the lushness of the hills. On both sides high velvet mountains rose straight out of the water. Rivulets cascaded down granite gullies and made puddly splashes in the channel.

They motored close to the bank where great ferns and mosses hung from the trunks of hemlocks. A huge salmon leapt and was gone, leaving a circle in the glass. An eagle from the aerie on the cliff swooped down to see if the Chris-Craft had flesh for her family. The sheet of water mirrored the banks exquisitely. For each sudden movement—each eagle lighting, each otter skittering—there was movement twice: once in real life and once in the inlet mirror. Laura caught Theo's eye and smiled at his expression. He said, "I had no idea this was here."

"The whole coast is like this, all the way up to Alaska."

Max guided them ceremoniously into the center of the channel, clearly enthralled with the shape and the feel of the ride. "Look how our wake sweeps out to both sides of the channel. I feel like we should have processional music." They rounded a bend and the fairy world ended, at least temporarily.

"Clear-cut," said Ho.

The mountainside straight ahead was a battlefield of naked stumps and sunburned ground cover. Shattered tree trunks lay like pickup sticks on the sandstone ridges and tracks of heavy equipment scarred the earth. At the upper edge of the clear-cut, the still-standing trees arced across the mountainside, showing a cycle-shaped rim of black shade, obscene access to the forest floor.

"That looks awful."

"Can't have everything," said Laura. "Lumber or scenery, take your choice." In her voice she heard echoes of Larry Todd: Five years earlier he had said the same thing to her. She found herself resenting his intrusion.

"Are the Indians doing this?" asked Ho.

"No," said Laura, "this is Crown land, belongs to the province. They lease it out to timber companies."

"So how is it that the Tsamians can lay claim to all this?"

"Except for some tribes in Quebec, Canadian Indians never signed treaties the way American Indians did. Essentially, whites just moved in and took over. I think the Tsamians can make a really good case that it's all theirs. The snafu is that if they claim it they have to give up their monthly government allowance and protected status. That's pretty scary stuff if you've counted on it all your life."

"I wish them well," said Max. He turned to Ho. "In his book Allessandro Siecetti used the quote about nature being a second mistress. Don't you feel her now?"

Laura broke in. "The dean has a book out?"

"Oh yes, quite recent. He's a philosopher, the book's on aesthetics."

"What's it called?"

"*Of Vivid Quality.* Evidently he discusses the use of vivid aesthetic experience in human adaptation. The study takes up where Jenkins left off."

"Maximilian, you read that in a review."

"You don't expect me to read the *book*, do you?"

"Of course not, only graduate students read books."

"Are the reviews good?" Laura asked.

"So far."

"I'm surprised an administrator has time to write," said Laura.

"He's not married, you know; that in itself frees up a lot of time. He's been invited to join our crowd several times, but he's one of those University of Chicago types and they tend to be a little standoffish—act like graduate school was some kind of boot camp for the brain.'' Ho took off his glasses and cleaned off dried salt.

"Siecetti's not American, is he?'' Laura asked. "He has that little bit of accent.''

"No, actually it's quite interesting. His father was a Roman journalist, anti-Mussolini. The whole family escaped in 1938 one step ahead of the *squadristi*. They lived in Switzerland for a while, then relocated to Illinois.''

They cruised past the clear-cut. Ten miles into the inlet they continued motoring east through the lush hills. The air, still holding rain, had changed from brisk and coastal to sweet and moist. Their bow was the only motion in the glass and the contrast between the high green banks and still, watery mirror was a sight the eyes could not tire of.

At the twelve-mile mark, the north bank broke open into a great glacial valley. Max steered to port, aiming for a dock where two gill-netters were tied. On a gentle slope above stood a row of yellow and white frame houses. Laura said, "Something you should know about Keena: They don't allow any beer; they don't even want to smell it on your breath.''

"Then we're in good shape; we have only scotch,'' said Max.

"No scotch either.''

Theo asked, "What did Robert Hunt mean about the Tsamians letting 'that woman' drive the fishing boat?''

"Probably nothing,'' said Laura. "Women don't drive boats.''

"But who is she? You knew who he was talking about and he didn't even say her name.''

"You'll meet her.''

CHAPTER 10

On the dock a mechanic's head popped up from behind an engine winched out of a gill-netter. Theo said, "In Louisiana, if you left your junk on the dock that way you'd start a fistfight."

"Nobody minds."

"It's a public dock, isn't it?"

"Public and private don't mean much here."

They docked easily and Laura leapt off with a bowline. Max cut the engine, and in the first moments of unnatural silence Laura savored Keena again. Keena, where time was measured by the light in the air and where life proceeded at the ceremonial pace called Indian time.

The mechanic stood up and, straightening his back, walked with a graceful swinging gait out to the end of the dock. His reflection flashed in the inlet mirror. Laura watched

Theo straighten his back, unconsciously imitating the Indian's stance.

The Indian smiled serenely at Laura. "Well, Laura Ireland, you aren't the policeman, is he the policeman?"

Laura wrapped her bowline quickly and hugged Uncle Joseph. "Hi, Uncle Joseph, good to see you. It's been a long time. And, yes, he's the policeman. He missed your mail boat by thirty minutes today."

Talbot stayed on the boat, clearly reluctant to take a false step. Uncle Joseph stared at the turtleneck under Talbot's chamois shirt and said, "Oh yes. I heard all about it after I got back here. Come on off if you're coming." He gestured. "You're welcome here."

Talbot stepped over to the dock and extended a hand. "Theo Talbot, Bellingham Police."

"I'm Joseph George. You'll be meeting my nephew John George, he's the chief. Or maybe Radiator, she does the typing."

"Radiator?"

"His wife." Uncle Joseph's black eyes searched Theo's face for reaction.

Max called from the bridge. "I'll be along in a minute, I want to enter this in the log. Ho is going to find our exact latitude coordinates."

Uncle Joseph looked at Max, then turned politely away.

Theo looked up to the village on the rise above the dock. It consisted of a dozen small houses in a single row facing the inlet; some had totem poles in front, others picket fences. Behind the houses was the community center: a double-wide mobile building surrounded by playground equipment.

Talbot turned to Laura. "Where are the cars?" he asked.

"No roads."

"How do they get around?"

They began walking up the hill. "On foot," she said. "Or with that." She pointed to a shiny black dirt bike lying by the dock. "But any place you really need to go, you go by boat."

"How many people live here?"

"Fifty or so."

"I had the impression Keena was much bigger."

"Really? I hadn't even heard of the place until Larry Todd brought me here."

"You still love Larry Todd, don't you?"

Laura was so surprised she stopped walking. "I don't know."

As abruptly as he had asked the question, Talbot changed the subject and began walking again. "Robert Hunt was right to say the Tsamians need Albert Bay. You couldn't run government services for a population of fifty."

"No."

"Still, this is a much different place from Albert Bay, it has a different feel. It feels like you're onstage here and someone important is watching your performance."

"It's the reflections," said Laura.

"Perhaps." Then he asked, "Is the woman's name really Radiator?"

"Tory for short. Her mother meant 'one who radiates.' The word resonates differently if you're not thinking about cars."

"Do you think her mother knows how it sounds to outsiders?"

"Actually, I've never met her mother. I heard she's an alcoholic and lives in Prince Rupert."

"And her father?"

"A Greek sailor from Vancouver."

As they approached the community center a rush of cold air blew by and Laura felt the first drops of new rain on her face. Inside the building a play group held forth in the big room. Stubby brown boys swarmed over a plastic slide while under a table, tiny girls told secrets into their cupped hands. A pregnant woman was in charge.

Laura walked up to the woman and asked, "Is Chief George here? We were wondering if he'd take us to the dig."

"Where do we go?" asked Max.

Chief John George sat in the swivel chair, admiring Max's digital bottom sounder. "Up-inlet a little farther, I'll show you the float when we get there." Still in his thirties, John George sported graying pigtails and a mouthful of denture-perfect teeth. His dark muscled hands clutched the arms of the swivel chair and he sucked on his upper plate as he watched Max at the wheel.

Max turned on his windshield wipers against the gentle rain and reversed in a big lazy swath out to the middle of the inlet. To John George he said, "Could you explain to me why archaeological digging is still going on when so much is already known. I found the Vancouver ethnology museum very complete."

"You seen that?"

"The architect's a friend."

"That right? Well, you can use new digging for all kinds of things. We're using ours in court in a few months to argue claim to the inlet and upriver to show that Tsamian lived here since precontact. The site that's covered over is dating between six hundred and one thousand years."

"How did it get covered?"

"Blowout, real common where there's fault lines, soil changes." He turned to Laura. "You don't know about the blowout last year. All of Cumcum Creek, the whole valley, come right down into the inlet."

"What's a blowout?" asked Ho.

"When the ground gets saturated higher it all lets go like the whole mountain's coming down. It's always happened— geologists can show you where old ones are—but it seems to be happening more these days with the logging."

"Can't someone make them be more careful?"

John George looked out at the inlet, now a vibrating surface of overlapping rain circles. "They can always try to do right by a place, but you can't tell what your problems are going to be until after you get started."

"Did the blowout hurt the dig?" asked Laura.

"The dig's fine. The new creek bed is about twenty yards closer, though."

Theo spoke up. "I have a question, John, totally unrelated. What's the possibility of someone up here being involved in Larry Todd's murder, somebody who might be threatened by your court case, something like that?"

John gave him an appraising look. "Tory and I talked about that one," he said after a moment. "We wondered if somebody from the government, or maybe a logging contractor, was trying to get back at us. But if it was somebody worried about Todd's working the dig, it still wouldn't make no sense to kill him. Everybody knows we could always get somebody else.''

"One more thing, John. After we told some folks over at Albert Bay that Todd was killed Saturday night they seemed to remember your coming into port real early Sunday morning.'' Talbot watched the Indian's face carefully.

John just shook his head. "Sounds like Timpkish. They know perfectly well we were fishing and the engine broke down.'' Looking steadily back at Theo, he said, "You know we're already feuding with them about them losing our artifacts, don't you?''

"You mean the museum theft last November? That was Tsamian stuff?''

"The best stuff was, the best stuff is always Tsamian. The hardest part is that Timpkish accused of us stealing it ourselves. And over here, we're about going crazy because they lost it. What kills you is they don't even care the stuff is gone, they just want money for a new museum.''

"Why was your stuff in their museum?''

John George made quick eye contact to see how much explanation Talbot really wanted. Looking away, he began: "About thirty years ago when the band was almost broken apart, Uncle Joseph brought the Hamatsa stuff over to Albert Bay. Hamatsa's real sacred, nobody but the men really should even be seeing it. Anyway, the government convinced everybody that the old culture was dying and everything should be in museums. Uncle Joseph wasn't the only one, everyone believed it. All the bands started turning in their things. Albert Bay museum was closest, so we took our stuff there.''

"I guess I still don't understand why everyone makes such a big deal over this stuff,'' said Theo.

John George smiled, happy for the honest question. "Maybe we can show you some stuff tonight. Tory's really good at it, she used to be a schoolteacher.''

"Okay, last question. What's the possibility of Larry Todd stealing the museum stuff?''

John George leaned forward. "As a matter of fact we think there might have been a lot of possibility. It wasn't public knowledge yet, but last month we asked Todd to leave the dig because we realized he had probably found a whole lot more stuff than he'd been telling us about. That got us wondering about him and the museum. But we couldn't really prove he stole from us, so how are we going to prove that he stole from the museum?''

Guiltily Laura used the distraction of passing out rain ponchos to get as far from John George as the bridge would allow. She thought of the cache of copper bracelets she had brought down to Bellingham for Larry; John George didn't even know they existed.

They motored eastward through the rain, into the heart of the great green mountains. Everywhere they spotted animals. Salmon leapt like an omen and curious gulls swooped overhead. Harbor seals swam in their wake while otters watched shyly from the rocks. Humans, it appeared, were the only animals who sought cover in the rain.

As they donned their rain ponchos John George pointed to a dock—a "float" he called it—in the cleft of two hills. The Chris-Craft puttered in and John George hopped off to help with docking.

The float was constructed of slippery fir planks and was anchored only a few yards from where a debris-strewn creek splashed noisily into the inlet. Over the din of the creek and the rain John George had to shout.

"Laura, you go up first. I'll take the rear, in case somebody slips."

Laura ducked through the hole in the dripping hemlock saplings and waited for the others to follow. Under the trees the rain was less a nuisance and in a moment her eyes adjusted to the shadows. Laura led them to a dirt stairway dug in the hillside. "Hold on to the handrails," she said as she grabbed one of the lashed-up saplings. "It's slippery."

The hillside dirt was sticky gray muck clearly destined for the bottom of the inlet in some near geologic time. They trudged up the tiny dirt steps, testing each for traction. Theo said, "In Louisiana we call this kind of mud 'gumbo.' It gets up under the fenders of the John Deere till she won't move. Working a gumbo field is like something out of Dante's hell."

"What do you grow?" asked Laura.

"Sugar cane."

"Can't you wait until the field dries?"

"No, ma'am." He was doing a Southern number on her. "Not at grinding time. You've got to keep working to get the cane out before frost comes."

As they neared the site Laura became more animated. "John, you've sunk the third hole. And it's dead center on the hearth. That's exactly where we thought it would be." She dragged John George over to tell her about the new site.

Ho, Theo, and Max stood panting in the rain, totally unimpressed with archaeology. The dig consisted of three squared-off pits dug deep into the muddy hillside. The biggest pit was ten-by-ten and the smallest five-by-seven. At their bottoms the pits were covered with tarps that collected rainwater. The only other indication that humans cared about the site were the two wooden shacks twenty yards away, their downhill sides propped on cinder blocks.

Laura turned to the men. "Isn't this exciting? I was so happy here." They said nothing. Rivulets ran down their faces. Refusing to be patronized, Laura said, "No, dummies, look. On this wall you can see where the gray mud ends and a tan layer begins. See, about three feet down? That's how deep the mud slide was; it just washed down and engulfed the village."

"That'll break up your bridge game."

"Ho, remind me not to take you to a dig again. Can we open the sheds, John?"

As John fumbled for his keys, he said, "Laura, I know you said you wanted to look for Larry's duffel but I can't ever remember him leaving it behind that way."

"But we can look."

They climbed the rickety steps and huddled inside. The tiny shed was lined with a U-shaped workbench. Every square inch of bench top was covered with bones, shells, and rocks laid in meticulous rows. Laura dropped to her knees to search under the bench. Talbot watched her movements closely. After a moment, she straightened and sighed. John George asked, "Any luck?"

"No. Darn it. I was sure it would be here when I couldn't find it in Bellingham."

"Want me to open the other shed?"

"Yes, please."

Theo Talbot again attached himself to Laura's side. As they neared the other shed they were hit by a blast of wet air from the creek. The shed was so close to the new creek bed the spray misted their faces. On its creek-side wall the shed wore a glistening carpet of moss. Rain dripped off both sides of the pitched roof.

"I used to go to sleep at night listening to the creek," Laura said. "But it was farther away back then."

"I had no idea conditions were so primitive," said Ho. "I don't think I would have let you go."

"It was fun."

"Some people find flagellation fun."

This shed was set up for sleeping. Along the sidewalls were Canadian Forces bunk beds, across the back, green gym lockers. Under a rickety table sat a new butane heater bearing a strip of masking tape that read "Todd." The sight of the heater made them all quiet for a minute.

John said, "Maybe you could bring that back for Barbara Todd; she might use it."

"I don't think she's the camping type, John."

"Oh no. She used to like it here. She'd come summers with Larry back when we were piping the houses, but that was before your time."

Theo Talbot opened one of the lockers on the back wall. Inside was a bent paring knife and a bag of salt.

"The lockers are too small for what we're looking for."

Laura climbed on a stool and peered into the rafters. She stood waiting for her eyes to adjust to the dark. Suddenly her stomach became queasy: looking up into the dark that way had a curious effect on her, as if the floor moved under her feet. She looked out the window and saw a tree go by. The floor really *was* moving, the whole shed was sliding down the hillside.

"It's the creek!" shouted John George. "Hang on!"

The shed door opened and they saw trees, bushes, rocks, gliding along beside them on a hillside turned to Jell-o. A huge tree trunk, wide as an auto body, floated past them down the hill. The heater, bunk beds, and table began sliding toward the door. Laura reached up for a rafter on which to brace herself; within seconds her hands were riddled with splinters.

From the corner of her eye Laura saw the gym lockers teeter. "Look out!" Theo called. He jerked Ho into a lower bunk. The heavy lockers crashed down on the spot where Ho had just stood. The table slid down the floor and smashed to bits against the doorframe. The pieces fell into the gray ooze and floated beside them. Then the butane heater slid quietly out the door and disappeared. Ho wrestled free of Theo's grip and tried to make a run for the door.

"Stop him!" shouted John. Theo grabbed Ho's rain poncho and, hand over hand, hauled him in. Everyone clung to bunk beds and wall studs for dear life.

Laura watched through the door as the inlet rushed forward in horrifying slow motion. The framed picture of water quietly filled her field of vision and a second later the shed splashed hard into the paralyzingly cold water. She yelled in astonishment as the icy salt water rushed in.

The cabin dipped under, rose and bobbed twice, then listed over on its back side at an angle. Water streamed over the threshold and in through the shuttered windows. By the time the frigid water was up to Laura's chest her body was numb. A quiet feeling in her head began to tell her it would be safer if she went to sleep. So this is how you die, she thought, you go to sleep to make it less cold.

A hard whack on her chest forced her to inhale and she screamed at feeling the cold again. Theo was treading water in front of her.

"Breathe," he ordered. "You weren't breathing."

The shed was so full of water it had righted itself and was now floating upright with only a foot of air near the ceiling. The doorway was no longer visible. Laura held very still. Every movement in the icy salt water felt like razor blades against her skin.

"Take off your poncho and get out," Theo ordered. He pointed to the door, a shining green hole below the waterline. Laura drew in a breath to duck under. Then she saw Ho.

"Theo, look!"

Bug-eyes and blue, Ho clutched a rafter in the corner. Acute distress was in his eyes.

Suddenly unmindful of the paralyzing cold, Laura treaded over and Theo followed. "He can't swim," she said over her shoulder.

"Make him breathe," said Theo. "He's holding his breath."

Laura slapped ineffectually around Ho's shoulders and back. "I can't get to his chest, he's hugging the rafter." Ho was losing his crazed expression; in seconds he would be passing out.

"Hit him in the gut, anything!" said Theo.

Inhaling deeply, Laura grabbed the rafter with both hands and ducked under water. Holding her arms straight to keep herself under, she pulled her feet up and kicked Ho hard in the stomach. Then, to be extra sure, she kicked him again. She popped to the surface to see Ho vomiting french fries and coleslaw down his chin. His glasses were knocked askew and one arm had let go of the rafter.

In her ear Theo urged, "Hold his glasses, I'll carry him."

Laura reached for the glasses and found that her hand would barely close around them. Her fingers were so cold she felt no sensation. It was like watching someone else's hand at work. Treading to the door, she did a surface dive and came up to see black patches outside—floating logs called deadheads. Finding a clear space in the flotsam, she shoved a log away to make sure Theo would have one too. But Theo didn't come.

"Theo!"

His muffled voice came from inside the shed. "He won't go under, he's fighting me."

Laura yelled, "Ho Kauffmann, you do what he says!"

There was no sound.

With her foot she shoved away the log again. Surprisingly, it was smooth and barkless: It had been entirely stripped while tumbling down the mountain. Behind her loomed the huge tangled roots of a floating cedar tree, as menacing as Medusa's hair.

"Theo?"

No sound, and the frigid salt water felt like acid on her

face. Finally white air bubbles rose beside her. Up came Theo clutching Ho in a lifesaving carry while Ho waved his arms wildly, fighting mad.

Behind them they heard John George's voice over the pinging of the rain. "Get out of the water quick." He and Max were perched on floating logs. "Water'll kill you faster than anything."

Poncho tangled around her legs, Laura treaded over to a floating trunk and climbed out of the icy water, exhausted and numb. Facedown on the log, she bit her finger to see if there was still feeling. Then she began biting hard on all her fingers, relieved to feel a slight tingle of pain.

Nearby, Theo helped Ho onto the base of a massive Douglas fir. The trunk bobbed and rolled as they both struggled to climb on. Laura shivered uncontrollably and watched them flounder; she would rather see them die than go in the frigid water to help. Finally Theo dragged Ho up and they clung mutely to the roots.

Laura scanned the floating raft of trees, looking for Max and John. Max had flung himself over a bobbing fir stump and was working hard to keep it from tipping over. John sat straddling a Douglas fir, his legs dangling in the water. The whole flotilla of debris moved slowly out from the shore toward the middle of the inlet. Laura found most distressing the huge bobbing tree roots; it was unnatural for them to be turned to the sky.

"Button and zip everything you got," called John. "I don't know how long we're going to be."

"I'll go for shore," yelled Max.

"You'll die first. Hold still till they come get us."

"How long?"

"Depends on whether they saw the wave sent down by the blowout."

Laura called to Theo, "How's Ho?"

"Shivering."

Ho's shaky voice piped up, "Do you have my glasses, Laura?"

"I tucked them in my waist."

Ho's voice came pitiful and small through the rain. "I'm sorry I was rude."

Laura looked across to Theo and asked him silently for the proper answer to a man in Ho's position. Finally she called, "You were a prince, Ho." Theo Talbot smiled at her weakly.

A boat horn sounded and they all turned in its direction. Around the point came the Georges' fishing boat, a woman's dark head visible on the bridge. "It's Tory," said John. "I was hoping they'd be down on the float." As the boat got closer they saw Uncle Joseph and two other men with gaff hooks standing on deck.

The fishing boat motored toward them, closer and closer to the ugly sea of logs. "Lordy, be careful with that prop," John George prayed to his wife.

As if listening to his words, Radiator cut the engine and let the boat glide the last hundred yards. The men with gaff hooks pushed away what they could from under the bow. The deadheads slowed their momentum and they ended up punting the last fifty yards, pushing themselves off tree stumps, moving the boat with sheer muscle power. Radiator dropped a rope ladder over the side. "Get the sling," yelled John. "Some of 'em can't climb."

Laura knew her life depended on getting to the sling. Afraid to waste an ounce of energy, she lay on the log, shivering silently, waiting for directions from the boat. When it was finally her turn, Uncle Joseph dropped the padded yellow loop in front of her face. The effort required to get the sling over her head and arms nearly made her pass out. They hoisted her carefully up to the rail and helped her climb over. By that time she didn't know if anyone else was still alive nor did she have the energy to care. A few minutes later she found herself curled in a fetal position under a blanket on the bridge deck. She heard Max's voice beside her. "My boat. Where's my boat?"

"Across the inlet." Radiator's voice came from above. "She floated free. We'll come back and get her later. We got to get you folks warm first."

"My boat—"

"We'll get her for you, don't worry."

Everyone in the village was waiting on the float. As each victim was bundled off the boat, a small knot of townspeople hustled him off to one of the houses. Laura was helped down into waiting arms. They were the arms of Uncle Joseph's wife, Rebecca. Relief flooded her eyes.

"You poor dear." The kindness was a cooing noise, a gentle urgent rush to get her up the hill. "We'll get you into a warm tub, dear. They're filling one for you now. Joseph, come help her up the hill, she can barely walk."

Laura had no memory after that. She lay in a bathtub, dimly aware of Rebecca entering occasionally to pour more hot water into it. It was lucky, Rebecca said, that only five people went into the inlet because there were only six tubs in Keena. But everyone in town, of course, was heating water on their wood stoves.

Finally Rebecca poured in a kettle of water so hot Laura's cheeks began to sweat. She stood up and Rebecca brought in Laura's satchel retrieved from the Chris-Craft.

After dressing, Laura went out on the porch and looked up and down the row of houses. The rain had stopped and dinner was cooking all over town. Laura felt clean and hungry, like after a shower in the gym. Theo came out of a house two doors down, wearing a red plaid shirt and jeans. He looked woodsy and handsome and she was surprised at how glad she was to see him.

He walked over. "How are you?" he asked. He seemed actually to care.

She held out her hands. "Splinters."

He took them in his own to examine them. "We can work on these later." They were standing close, so they moved apart.

"How's Ho?" she asked.

"They said he's fine, he went down to the Chris-Craft to be with Max. You and I are supposed to eat at the Georges."

"It's down at the end, I'll show you."

"They filled my tub with a kettle from the stove," Theo said.

"The houses were only piped about ten years ago, hot water is asking a bit much."

In the Georges' front yard they were met by a ten-foot welcoming figure: a carved cedar humanoid with outstretched arms and a wide-open mouth. Crowning the figure was a magnificently painted raven with a hooked beak and open wings. On the porch three black-haired girls were jumping off and twirling in the air before landing. They stopped the game when Laura and Theo walked up.

"Are your mother and father here?" Theo asked.

The girls didn't answer. He turned to Laura. "Do they speak English?"

"Mommy is over at Moma's getting the food. Are you the people who's eating here?" The question was asked by the oldest, a pretty, serious girl with thin braids down her back.

"Yes, we are," said Laura. "You're Amanda, do you remember me?"

"I don't know."

"You got big, and you have braces on your teeth."

Amanda's delicate eyebrows wrinkled. "Daddy says I have to have them when I go to school with white kids." Then she reddened, realizing Laura was white.

"Do our other friends know to eat here?"

"They wanted to eat on their boat."

"Oh dear. I bet they were too tired to be nice guests, I'll explain to your mother."

"We're not eating here anyway, we're eating at Moma's."

"Who's Moma?" asked Theo.

"John's mother, she cooks for the whole family so Tory doesn't have to keep a stove going."

"We're going to sleep there too, so you can sleep in our room," Amanda said.

"Thank you."

"We like to sleep at Moma's. She makes popcorn, and clothes for our Barbies."

"Ah."

A new voice piped up. "I got a Barbie too."

Laura and Theo turned to the little ones. As beautifully dark as their big sister, they wore their hair cropped short with bangs. They had on jeans and plaid shirts and the younger one had a fan-shaped wet spot around her crotch; Laura could smell her now.

Radiator George came from the house next door with a casserole dish in her hands. Theo stopped in his tracks and just stared at her: Radiator George was a stunningly beautiful woman. She was dark and shining with almond-shaped eyes that smiled without trying. Her hair was silky black. Curving bangs framed her cheekbones and eyes. She was alive and smiling and glowed with love. As she tilted her head, the silken fringe swayed and caught light. She said to Laura, "You're looking much better. How do you feel?"

"Much better!"

"We thought we would put you in the girls' room? Do you mind?"

"Not at all."

"Come on in."

The two of them followed Tory into the little living room. Aging furniture was covered with afghans and throws, and a row of potted plants caught the light under the long front window. "Theo, I hope the sofa's big enough. Laura, why don't you bring your things back now? I'll make sure the girls have their stuff out of the way."

Back in the bedroom Laura opened her briefcase to get a hairbrush. As Tory cleared away stuffed animals she said, "I'm so glad to see you with a boyfriend, Laura. I used to worry about you, so tall, and liking Larry so much."

Laura brushed her hair.

CHAPTER 11

Laura bent over to look into the little girls' mirror. Boyfriend? Of course Tory was talking about Theo Talbot. In the mirror her eyebrows were standing straight up so she brushed them down with her fingertips. She quickly plaited her braid.

Out in the kitchen, Laura found Theo and Tory chatting like old friends. Tory finished her story: "So by the time I got to university I was telling people my name was Victoria and I was from Hong Kong. I wore a quilted silk jacket and lots of fake jade."

Theo said, "I know what you mean, I never say mine any place north of Baton Rouge. I mean, who's going to believe your momma'd call you 'Toe-feel'?"

"What?" asked Laura.

"My name is Theophile Talbot, at home I'm Toe-feel. They started calling me Theo in the seminary."

"You were in the seminary?"

"Only for a while. I stayed with the Jesuits after college so I wouldn't have to go home and grow sugar cane. I wouldn't have made a very good Jesuit."

"Why not?"

"Well, the crowning reason was that I walked out in the middle of something called the Long Retreat and bought a ticket to a Woody Allen film festival. Everybody, including me, knew it was an unsubtle way of saying I don't want to be here."

John George came in with his sleeves rolled up, engine grease to his elbows. Holding his arms out, he kissed Tory without otherwise touching her, then began lathering his hands with cleaning solvent from a jar above the sink.

"Boat fixed?" asked Theo.

"Almost."

"What's the problem?"

"Cracked piston. We decided to change rings and grind the valves while we were at it."

"Is that the boat Tory skippered into Albert Bay Sunday morning?"

"She wasn't driving."

Tory said, "I was probably helping out on the bridge while they were towing. Come on, everyone, let's eat while the food is hot."

She shuffled them to a high-backed breakfast nook with a narrow plank table. "Laura, why don't you and Theo sit across from each other at the girls' end? John and I need to sit here so we can get out."

Laura looked at Theo. She knew what would happen if they tried to fit their legs in across from each other in the narrow booth. An amused smile broke over Theo's face. "Our hostess is waiting," he said. Laura folded herself into the small space and waited for Theo on the other side. He slid in and expertly wedged one of his knees between hers so their legs were intertwined.

Tory took the lid off a noddle casserole and offered it to Laura. As delicately as possible Laura took one quarter of the food.

"I hope we have enough for you," said Tory.

"I just didn't want to worry about seconds."

Theo followed her lead. They ate like people who had just left most of their body heat someplace else.

After a few minutes of famished eating Theo took a drink of water and asked, "Is it true Larry Todd didn't have any students with him at the dig this year?"

Tory nodded. "I'm afraid so. There were two girls last summer that we thought would be digging fall weekends, but in September they didn't come."

"Did he say what happened?"

"Just said they quit."

"So on weekends he'd come by himself?"

"Yes, at first. Then he started skipping some, then a lot. By December he was hardly coming at all, and when he did, he would just hang around the work shed, even on clear weekends. It was really kind of sad, but we didn't know what to say. Finally, we ended up asking him to leave, but that was for other reasons."

"I already told them about that," John said.

The food was gone in minutes. John pushed his plate away and sucked at his teeth. "Did you still want to see some Tsamian stuff or did the dip in the inlet wear you out?"

"You don't mind taking things down?" asked Laura.

"No, I need to get used to my blanket again. Rebecca's been adding things to it and I need to make sure it's not too heavy to dance in."

"What did she do to it?" asked Laura.

"Sewed on some copper feathers. They stick out the back."

"Interesting," said Laura. "That must be heavy."

"It is."

Theo said, "There's aluminum on the market that's about one quarter the weight."

"Lightness isn't the issue," said Laura. "Copper was a very valuable material in the old days, the most valuable—like gold for whites. In fact, the ultimate object for a coastal chief to own was a shield made entirely of beaten copper. There were so few of them they even had names."

Tory added, "Our most important copper was stolen from the Albert Bay museum in November. It was called Moon

Man Eyes and had been around so long no one remembers its whole story. We were just devastated; losing something like that is like losing part of yourself. Since November we've really broken off with the Timpkish; we now realize we can't rely on anyone but ourselves.'' She turned to John. ''If you're going to dress you should do it now, these people will be very tired soon.''

Laura slid out of the booth. ''May I get Ho and Max? I know they want to see this.''

John began dragging boxes out from behind the couch. ''Go ahead, Laura, I'll get started with the policeman here.''

From a cardboard box John took an oversized wooden bird on a handle and held it out. ''Okay, this is Raven, it's a rattle. It's carved entirely from one piece of hollowed-out cedar, even the handle.'' John held it belly side up and shook. Pebbles rattled inside.

Theo smiled. ''May I?''

John presented him with the handle.

Theo examined the delicate abalone shell inlay on the smooth wooden belly. At the anus he noticed a plugged hole where the pebbles had been inserted. Turning it over, he admired the bird's back. ''The wings are carved to look like they're folding in.''

''Yes.''

''The way you hold a bird so it can't fly away.''

''Yes.''

Each feather was crosshatched and distinct. Differences between flight feathers and covert feathers were exquisitely distinguished. John reached over and turned the rattle belly side up in Theo's hand. ''You're really not supposed to hold him right side up. He might fly away.''

''Oh.''

The eye-shaped abalone inlay shone like fathomed water. ''The eye design seems to be on everything,'' said Theo. ''What's it for?''

''Just design,'' said John. ''Some people say eyes give a piece more power, more ways to see.''

Theo wanted to see the wings again and tried to peek at the underside. John stirred uncomfortably, then gently took Raven away.

Next John took out a wool cloak of black-and-red Tsamian design outlined in pearly white shirt buttons. On one edge, beaten copper feathers protruded from the fabric. John draped the cloak over his arm and picked up the Raven rattle. Then he left the room.

"What's he going to be when he comes out?"

"Raven, spirit of his clan. John's family has all the privilege stories associated with Raven."

"I don't understand what that means."

Light caught the shining veil of Tory's hair as she raised her lovely chin. "It means that there is no one else on earth right now who has the right to wear the Raven costume, or tell the family's stories. The stories are the most important thing we own. All I can think to compare them with is your family photographs, but of course, they're much more serious than that."

"Why did they choose a raven? I can think of a lot more impressive animals—killer whales, eagles . . ."

"You Americans and your eagles. Ravens are much more important than eagles. They're certainly much smarter; they might even be the smartest creature. They're like dolphins in the way they know your mind: You must keep a pure heart when you're with a raven."

"That so?"

"Absolutely. For instance, sometimes when you're out in the woods by yourself a raven will start following you around. He'll sit watching from a tree and very quickly get to know your heart. Sometimes he'll caw at you to show you something beautiful or swoop down from behind if you're not paying enough attention to him. And if you stay out there a long time, lost in your own thoughts or troubles, do you know what he'll do?"

"What?"

"Play a joke."

"Oh God, a bird?"

"Yes, he'll drop a clam shell on your head, or laugh at you when something—"

The bedroom door opened and Raven stepped out. He wore a huge wooden mask with a curved beak. His black-

and-red robe rippled with light reflected from the shirt buttons. The copper feathers shivered.

On the mask Raven's inlay eyes stared at all viewers no matter which way he turned his head: A tilt one way made white skyholes, a tilt the other shot off rays of reflected light. Theo's eyes jumped back and forth from the undulating robe to the knowing eyes. Raven shook rattles and started a chant from within the mask just as Laura walked in with Ho and Max.

Raven did not speak. Gesturing for them to sit, he checked his plummage, then shuffled a few tentative steps.

Suddenly an opening plaint rose up from behind Raven's mask. His song was not so much music as laryngeal yearning, a plainsong for life. Sadness rose from Raven's throat, lonely and meterless, waveringly sweet. It enveloped the listeners and told about some part of life left long neglected. No world mattered except the lost one Raven sang of, no hurt—past or present—could not be assuaged.

Raven danced and chanted, showing off his feathers and beak. The watchers could see John's bare legs below the blanket but he still was not John. Raven chanted low, then high, pulling in air at random intervals.

When Theo looked around he saw the entire audience sat as motionless as he. Max, Ho, and Laura all watched silent and staring. Tory, too, sat erect and still as Raven's wing passed close to her face.

For twenty minutes Raven shook his feathers, dipped and turned. He chanted and flew with his red-and-black wings, seeing all from the eyeholes of light. Finally he dipped deeply to the floor and chanted with renewed voice, demanding their attention: He had decided to stop and was building for a climax. Crouching low, he let his voice become smaller and smaller. The mesmerized audience bent forward, breaths held, straining to keep Raven's voice alive. Something now would happen, something terrible about Raven. Suddenly, with a heartrending cry, Raven stood up and stopped singing. Stricken, they stared at his face. Slowly the mask began to open: Raven would show them his innermost secret. An eye, thought Theo, inside's an eye.

Inside was a human face, a carved Tsamian face, simple

and unadorned, the face of all humanity. Raven showed it quickly to everyone, closed the mask, and left the room.

After a moment's silence Tory got up and went to the bedroom. Ho and Max quietly said good night and left for the boat. Laura excused herself. In the girls' room, she undressed and dragged the girls' mattresses to the floor, listening to Theo move around out in the living room and bath. There was a knock on her door.

"Laura? I've got some alcohol and a needle, want to work on those splinters?"

"Just a minute." She put a sweatjacket over her camisole. "Come in."

Theo walked in and looked around. "You're sleeping on the floor."

Laura sat on the floor. "Tory suggested it, the beds are too short." She held her hand out to him. "My right hand's the worst." Sitting beside her, Theo swabbed her hand with an alcohol pad and began picking at the skin with a needle. His eyes narrowed in concentration.

The girls' room was shabby and familiar. Dolls and animals littered the corners and the blankets were pilled from too much washing. A faint urine scent rose from the mattresses and blended with the bleachy smell of the sheets.

Theo said, "I don't think I've ever been this close to little girls before."

"They're nice, aren't they?"

Theo glanced at a pair of stale panties stuffed under the dresser. "I guess I expected them to smell better—like baby women or something."

"Theo, you're so funny."

"You said my name."

"Is that the first time?"

"Think so."

He worked in the pool of yellow light cast by the naked bulb. Their breathing mingled in a warm pool.

"You were pretty nasty to me the first time we met," Laura said softly.

"Was I? It's hard to tell how other people view police routine."

"That was routine?"

"Can't leave a situation until you get what you came for."

"But I haven't done anything."

"Maybe not, but you have to admit, you've got yourself mixed up in some pretty ugly stuff."

"I'm not mixed up. I know enough about what's going on to stay away from the bad parts."

"And these bad parts, where might they be?"

"The Fat Cat, the Nammish Reservation, not here certainly; I feel perfectly safe here."

"Nice of you to say."

She decided not to explain it was Keena itself that made her feel safe, not his presence. "John's dancing gave me a really funny feeling tonight. I've never felt that way watching him before."

"Not your casual evening at home."

"Did you feel it too, that terrible sweet pit in your stomach?"

"Yes."

"I don't understand the dynamics. What do you suppose was happening out there?"

"Well, let's see, for one thing, his singing was very haunting and the bare legs made him vulnerable. And for another thing, he was seducing his wife."

"He what?" She quickly lowered her voice, remembering that John and Tory were in the next room. "How do you know that?"

"I'm older than you."

"You are not. How old are you?"

"Twenty-nine."

Laura was silent.

"A third thing," said Theo, "was that we probably contributed as audience: three couples, two of whom understood what was going on. Straighten your finger out."

"Three couples?"

His head was very close as he worked in the warmth between them. Laura felt his breath on her hands. "Theo, you just called us a couple."

"Last splinter," he said. Laura pulled her hand away and glared.

"It was a terrible mistake," he said. "Rotten thing to do,

especially considering what I'm going to do now." He reached in his pocket and clamped a pair of handcuffs to the bunk bed frame. Grabbing her wrist firmly, he clamped the second cuff on her.

"What's this for?" she demanded.

"I'm bringing you back on the mail boat first thing in the morning. You're going to be cited for entering a crime scene, maybe two. We can forget about citing you for leaving town without permission."

"You bastard—"

"I'll say."

"You mangy bastard."

"Laura, listen to me, this is the only way I know to get you off the streets. I'm really sorry it had to be like this, please try to get some sleep."

Theo pulled a mattress off the upper bunk and laid it outside her door. "Good night," he said, "I'll be right outside if you need anything."

"Theo Talbot, come in here and take these *OFF*."

"Laura, quiet down, you'll wake the Georges."

"*TAKE THEM OFF.*"

"I'd like to, but we both know you'd start wandering into things again. Heaven knows what trouble you'll get yourself into. Good night."

"What am I going to do, attack you in the night? You wish."

She heard him settle down on the mattress outside, refusing to answer. She decided to change her tack. "Well, I hope you're proud of yourself, Talbot. Big man, chaining a woman to bed." She jangled the cuffs. "Do you chain all your women to the bed?"

"For God's sake, you're not chained to a bed."

"I don't know what you call *this*." She jingled her wrist. "*This* is a chain." She rattled the bed. "*This* is a bed. I'm speaking English, I swear I'm speaking English."

"Laura, I'm sorry. It's just that I don't trust you."

"Trust *me*? How about the other way? It looks to me like I can't trust you." Thoughts of betrayal brought indignant tears to her eyes. "I thought you might even turn out to be a friend, and now look what's happened." Tears reminded her of Larry. "Why does this always happen to me?" She hid her face in a pillow.

Theo sat on the mattress outside the door listening to her buried sobs. The Georges' bedroom door opened a crack and Tory peeked out, looking an accusation at Theo.

Theo got up and went into the little girls' room. Sitting on a bed frame, he watched Laura on the floor search for hidden places on her sweats to dry her tears: the inside of hems, hood, and pockets.

"Laura, I feel as if I finally got your attention."

Refusing to look at him, she fought back a new wave of tears. "Boy, I'll say."

"Look, I've got you down for three misdemeanors. They aren't really important to me but I'm using them to keep you off the streets until we can clear up the two homicides. Is that clear?"

"But I'm not doing anything. I'm not in any danger." She remembered being shot at Wednesday, but this was not the time to mention it.

"May I give you a speech?"

"I don't care."

"I know you're operating from a different agenda, but for me this is a criminal investigation—no, more serious, this is a homicide investigation: two murders. What we know about people who are not simple spouse-killers is that they are high-statistic for killing again. If you stick your nose in this, you may be killed."

"*You're* sticking your nose in."

"It's what I get paid for, it's in the job description."

In a minute Laura said, "Okay, I appreciate what you're saying and I'll try to stay out of the way. Will you take these things off?" Her voice was meek.

"What will you do if I take them off?"

"Go to sleep; go to Seattle tomorrow."

"Straight to Seattle?"

"Yes."

After a moment Theo took a tiny set of keys from his pocket and opened the cuffs. Laura leapt up and went to the corner to rub her wrist.

Theo stood too and regarded her gravely through a bunk bed frame. "I'm sorry I got you so rattled."

She waved him away. "You can go. I didn't mean what I said about attacking you, or your chaining me to the bed."

"I was trying to do what I thought right."

"Sure. Makes perfect sense: You call us a couple, then chain me to a bed."

"Laura?"

"Please just go."

"I'm not supposed to leave until you're finished crying, handbook says so."

"You're not on duty. Go away."

He watched her as she worked at mastering the furious tears which welled again in her eyes. Shaking his head sadly, he said, "And I thought it would all be different when I left the seminary."

"What would? What seminary?"

"Jesuits have what they call the Rule of Touch: You keep a space barrier between you and everybody else, nobody's allowed to touch. It's a good rule at a boys' school, keeps down the buggery and fistfights. When I left, I thought one of the nice things would be touching people again. Maybe I overdid it for a while, but now, here we are: You need some arms around you and there's about a thousand different reasons why I can't get near. Father Murray strikes again."

"It would have been okay if you hadn't called us a couple."

"It just came out."

"Well, are we or aren't we?"

"I don't know."

"Theo, I can't get involved with a man who lives fifteen hundred miles away."

"It's not my idea of a good plan either."

"Is that an insult?"

"Laura, I'm just saying these things end up having a life of their own."

"Nice line, Talbot."

"Well, maybe I'm less worried about the fifteen hundred miles because I know something about us you don't."

They regarded each other carefully. Laura was the first to

turn away. "You actually think there's going to be some other time, don't you?"

"Laura, what would you do if I kissed you right now?"

"I don't know."

"But you wouldn't try to break my nose or anything?"

"No."

"You sure?"

Laura nodded.

Theo was across the room in two steps. "Give me your wrists." He brought the right one up to his mouth and kissed the soft skin on the underside. "I'm sorry I hurt you."

"It's okay."

In a rush of heat and want Theo leaned his whole weight against her, pressing her to the wall. Still holding her wrists, he raised them up and pinned her arms above her head. They kissed deeply, and for a long time. In a while their arms dropped and Theo slid his hands down her backside to pull her hips to him. They kissed again.

"Talbot, we can't do this."

"But we are."

"But we can't—"

"Honest-to-God copulation doesn't concern me right now." He brushed his mouth against hers. "This conversation is about something different."

"What then?"

"It's about 'how close.' "

"Is that what they taught you in the seminary?"

"Never got to pastoral counseling."

Laura's face clouded. "Wait a minute, I have to tell you something."

"What's that?"

"I don't have a very big bust."

"As a matter of fact, I've already practiced the perfect answer if you ever said anything. I'd say, 'Hey, Laura, no problem; my chest is pretty flat too.' "

"So you don't care?"

"Laura, before we were so rudely interrupted we were trying to figure out how close to the flame I get to hover."

"Are we talking about sex?"

"We're talking about whatever you want to talk about."

"So you're not interested in sex?"

"I didn't say that."

"Are you?"

"You bet your Nikes."

"I might be too, but not tonight, I'm not ready to think about it yet."

"Your choice," he said.

"We can't tonight anyway because I'd get pregnant."

"Sorry, no hiding behind that. If we're serious we can al—"

"I know perfectly well what we can and can't do. But I'm not ready tonight, I'd want to talk about it first, make you understand more about me."

"Talk."

"Well, if we do ever decide to make love I'd need for you to go slow enough—"

"Hey, you two." It was John George, his voice coming through paper-thin walls. "Look on the top shelf in the bathroom. But be quiet, you hear?"

Theo went out the bathroom and came back with a little packet. He began unbuttoning his shirt. "A sign from God," he whispered.

"What?" Laura whispered back.

"Condoms."

Afterward they were quiet, Theo wide awake, Laura almost dozing. He held her as close as bodies would allow, knowing for certain now that grace could be transferred through the skin. Running his hand over the toned muscles of her back and arm, he hit her bullet scab. She jolted awake.

"What's this?" he said.

"Somebody shot at me Wednesday in the park. Theo, I thought it might be you. It wasn't, was it?"

"No, it wasn't me." Fear shot both ways through Theo's spine. Whoever the killer was, he now had the power to inflict personal wounds. That was the problem with loving. Theo lay very still as Laura wrapped her arms around him and settled down with a contented sigh.

"Laura, two people have denied that Tory drives the boat, why do they do that?"

"Women don't skipper boats here."

"I'm a trained observer. I saw her."

"Show-off. So am I. In this culture if you see a woman skipper you're supposed to say she's only helping out. It's a perfect example of the difference between ideal and real behavior. White culture has a bunch of them too; I'm just too tired to think of any."

"Another thing: What happens to the dig now?"

"It'll be all right. I don't think the blowout was that close."

"I don't mean that. I mean, who takes it over now that Todd is dead?"

Laura pondered the question. "Maybe Dr. Buchanan will offer. He doesn't do his field anymore."

"Why not?"

"He's an Egyptologist and he's not supposed to go abroad anymore; intestinal virus nearly killed him last time. Don't hog the sheet."

"Sorry. One more question and I'll let you sleep. Barbara Todd seems to know an awful lot about buying and selling Indian stuff. How do I know she wasn't in on this smuggling?"

"With Larry? Don't count on it. When I was in Bellingham things were so bad between them he'd leave her notes on the fridge rather than talk to her. Lots of nights he'd sleep in the station wagon rather than go home. It wasn't what I'd call an ideal marriage."

Laura became silent again and her breathing grew deep and regular. Theo reached up to the bunk bed and quietly pulled down the handcuffs. Rolling Laura on her back, he cuffed her left wrist to his right one. Protesting in her sleep, she brought her arm up to her face. Instantly Theo followed with his own. She didn't wake and settled again into deep contented sleep. Theo settled his face close to hers and breathed in her sweet sleeping air.

CHAPTER 12

In the early morning Laura woke up with a pain in her wrist.
When she saw the handcuffs she realized she'd been wrong
about a man for the second time in her life.

Under the sheets Theo was naked; his clothes lay in a
pile on the floor. So where were the keys? Laura peeled back
a corner of his pillow and he stirred. She put it down gently,
waiting for his face to relax.

Under the chest of drawers Laura spotted a piece of or-
thodonic headgear, a black elastic skull piece hooked to a
steely smile. Reaching over her head, she snagged the headgear and began to probe under Theo's pillow with the steel
curve of the braces. Softly she checked the upper corners,
the lower ones, then in the middle, under his head. The prob-
ing didn't disturb him, but she wasn't finding keys either.

Next she snuggled close to check the far side of his mattress. Pushing the wire hook under the mattress corner, she

flicked her wrist. Two small keys slid across the linoleum floor. She tensed, but Theo didn't wake. Pulling the keys in gently, she tucked them under her own mattress.

After a moment she took out the keys, sat up noiselessly and worked one into the cuff. Looking around, she took a deep breath—ready, set, click. Up, she grabbed her blue sweats and moved silently through the kitchen, snatching the warm-ups drying by the stove. There was a soft noise back in the bedroom. The kitchen door banged behind her.

Laura ran down to the dock, naked as a spring day, clutching clothes to her chest. In the garden Grandma George was transplanting tomatoes. She looked up as Laura ran by.

"Good morning, Mrs. George."

On the path to the dock Uncle Joseph came toward her, his head bowed as he trudged up the hill. He heard her and looked up.

"Sorry, I'm in a hurry."

Up on the hill a door slammed. "Laura, come back."

She untied the Chris-Craft, pushed it away from the dock, and jumped on. From the cabin below came a surprised, "Who's there?"

"It's me, Max." She looked back to make sure the boat had floated away from the dock. " 'Open up quick, it's an emergency." Agitated voices echoed down the hill.

The Chris-Craft hatch opened to show a bleary-eyed Max wearing a sleeping bag around his waist. Laura snatched the boat key off the bulkhead and ran to the bridge. Theo Talbot, wrapped in a bed sheet, came running down the hill. "Laura, wait—"

At midships hung three borrowed Tsamian boat bumpers. Climbing down from the bridge, Laura unclipped the first one. From the dock Theo called, "Laura, listen to me—" In reply, she threw a fat rubber bumper at his head and bent down to undo the next. "For God's sake, Laura, at least put on some clothes." The second bumper she aimed at his feet, to keep him off guard. He dodged it and said, "Laura, you don't understand. I cuffed you to keep you out of trouble." Unclipping the third buoy, she stared directly in Theo's eyes and made a simple chest pass of the buoy. She ran up and started the engine to drown his voice.

Reversing out to the middle of the inlet, she put the boat in high gear and headed out to the coast. Steering one-handed, she pulled on her clothes. Off her bow, a boat was approaching Keena village. It was a red pleasure boat not belonging to the Tsamians. Throttling down, Laura unzipped the vinyl side window. The skipper of the other boat slowed down too and waved cheerily as he politely navigated her portside. "That's Barry Cunliffe!" she cried. Turning around, she read *Jolly Roger* off the stern just as Max arrived on the bridge, still pulling on his sweater.

"Who is he?"

"A really flaky guy who was one of Larry's graduate students before I was."

"What's he doing here?"

"I don't know. I didn't even know he had a boat."

"And what in heavens name happened on the dock back there with our young man?"

"Theo Talbot handcuffed me to the bed last night."

"Oh dear. And things got a little out of hand, did they?"

"That's not it. He wants to arrest me."

"Dear girl, what have you done?"

"Nothing. He was showing off."

Ho Kauffmann came up to the bridge, looking for an explanation.

Laura said, "We're leaving in a hurry because Theo Talbot wanted to take me in today and I haven't done anything."

Max raised an eyebrow at Ho. "He handcuffed her to the bed last night."

"He did? Well, Maximilian, it appears I am your debtor this time."

"I'll take it in chits, Doctor."

Laura was dumfounded: "You guys *bet* on us?"

"Max said the man was meatball for you. I said, 'Of course, that was obvious,' but you never can count on women to pursue the obvious." Ho bent to tie his Topsiders. "We didn't have time to talk last night but I'm still concerned about those letters you haven't found, Laura. How much trouble can they really cause you?"

"Plenty." Laura's voice was glum.

"But only if they fall into the wrong hands. And right now it would appear they are irretrievably lost."

"I don't think so. And I have another idea about where they could be."

Max looked to the heavens. "Dear God, don't let her say Juneau."

"No," she said. "Barbara Todd's."

Ho asked, "What makes you think your letters are there? You yourself said Todd spent very little time at home."

"I've looked in all the places Larry usually went. Now I've got to try the unusual places. Once when I was invited to their house I saw the duffel stuffed under his desk in the den. I bet it's there right now. Barbara's bound to go through that stuff and find my letters; she's the one person in the world who could really wipe me out."

"How?"

"By doing what Larry threatened: Tell my adviser I took artifacts from the dig. Ho, I've been thinking about this a lot since Larry telephoned me and I realized I wouldn't be able to function as an anthropologist if I knew somebody could blow the whistle on me at any time. I mean, why even start? I just couldn't live that way."

"Why would Barbara Todd want to hurt you?"

"Barbara hates me. Besides, there's another thing about Barbara that somebody ought to look into. Theo Talbot told me that there's a third person involved in Larry's murder and Barbara is the one who benefits financially from Larry's death. But, then, if that's true, what's Barry Cunliffe doing here?"

"Very well, confused one, what's the single best thing we can do for you when we get back?"

"Just drop me off at Barbara's. I promised Theo I would leave town and I will. As soon as I check Larry's den."

Max stood up to take the wheel from Laura. "My dear, I must say I admire your enlightened self-interest but, you know, that wasn't just a lovers' quarrel you had last night. That young man is quite enterprising. No doubt he's on the shortwave, even as we speak. They'll be waiting for us back in Bellingham."

"I'll go in disguise. I can put on my costume again."

Ho said, "You think Barbara Todd will give love letters to someone dressed as the Duke of Windsor?"

Max ignored him. "I'm worried about a much more salient problem. Both Ho and I have reason to keep the Bellingham police at a decent distance, and you, Laura, seem to be doing your best to provoke them. How do I know they won't confiscate my boat?"

"We won't dock there," Laura said decisively.

"Really?"

"We'll dock in Vancouver and rent a car, I'll pay for it with my Visa. Ho, we can put on our party clothes."

"I will not. I refuse to get arrested as an accessory to whatever this is."

Max shook his head. "At this point I must intervene. "Your costumes yesterday were amateurish to the extreme. If you insist on taking a role, Laura, I insist on providing mise-en-scène."

"Then you think it's a good idea?"

"I think it's the worst idea I've ever heard. But if you've decided that you must carry it through, I will make sure it is at least carried through professionally. Downtown Vancouver can provide us with all we need to turn you into a very pretty young man." His eyes appraised Laura. "I thought you had the potential yesterday, even without a chest wrap."

"What's a chest wrap?"

"Old theater trick. One encases the female torso in an Ace bandage to distribute the breast tissue across the entire rib cage; one can eliminate a whole bosom that way." Max patted her hand and looked again to the Straits of Georgia.

Ho said firmly, "I'm *not* dressing."

"And I see no reason to involve you, Doctor," Max said serenely. "This is Laura's scene; we can only help her play it."

Laura awoke to the stink of hot tar and diesel fumes. Outside the porthole were the docks of Vancouver. She climbed to the bridge for their entry into False Creek, standing by Max and Ho to watch their soft wake rock the covey of international pleasure boats. They puttered the last fifty feet into the visitors dock and Ho hopped off smartly with a bowline.

"My God," said Max as they tied up, "they charge more for a day here than a week at home."

"I'll pay for it, Max."

"Nonsense." He found the harbormaster's office and paid the fee, then hailed a cab for the Robson Street shopping district.

Max led them past places where rock music blared from storefronts and slick shiny boys lounged against lampposts. They walked slowly up and down the streets as Max scrutinized businesses, then finally stopped in front of one with a chrome façade and neon palm trees in the window.

In the gleaming white interior a male receptionist sat behind the desk wearing nerd sunglasses. "Yes," said Max firmly, "this is what we want."

Inside, harpsichord music tinkled from speakers; Max smiled as if it were a good sign. Positioning himself in front of the desk he talked loudly about Theatre, ignoring the nerd. Finally the shop owner left the head he was styling to come over. He and Max acknowledged each other as kindred spirits.

Max took Laura's arm. "This dear girl is starring in my production of *St. Joan*. We wish a tasteful short cut for her. Can we get that here?"

"Certainly. When's she opening?"

"Next week, at the Playhouse." Max picked up Laura's topknot. "Look here, I want a great hank saved on top that we can gel back. On the sides you must layer it *short-short*." Then he swept Laura's hair off her cheek to show the tendrils by her ear. "Leave these; they'll make *darling* sideburns and give the makeup man something to play with."

"I'll see if I can get someone on it."

"I want *you* to do it; now would be best. My choreographer," Max pointed to Ho, "meets with a Japanese dance company in one hour." Ho Kauffmann buried his nose in a magazine. The stylist glanced at the head in his chair. "I'll see what I can do."

Max beamed and walked around at the stylist's elbow.

"She's *exactly* what Shaw had in mind for Joan, don't you think?"

"I'm sure."

"What a well-run shop, I *must* bring my other actors here . . ."

An hour later Laura sat in the boat cabin, peering into a vanity mirror. Her head felt so light she thought she would float away. Her face looked leaner and her cheekbones more prominent. She saw the pearl studs in her earlobes and began to take them off.

"Your ring, too." Ho turned to Max. "How about her plastic watch?"

"Wrong color blue. When you finish there, dear, take off your upper clothing and hold this against your chest." He gave her the end of a thick Ace bandage to put over her rib cage. "Now, sit down and hold your arms up. You may rest you hands on your head if you like, this takes a while." Max unrolled the bandage around Laura's thorax, humming tunes from *Cats*.

"This is working out quite well, dear, your shoulders are very muscular."

"I know."

"Frankly," he said, "I prefer a torso like yours. Theatrically speaking, it's much more versatile than the dowager style: those dreadful hanging organs. When you need ballast on a female it's always easier to add than to subtract."

"You really know how to cheer a gal up."

"My pleasure."

"Max, I'm sorry we let Theo Talbot on the boat yesterday. I wasn't thinking about how uncomfortable that was for you."

"Entirely forgotten. Ho and I have discussed it already."

"Did it have something to do with Ho's Christmas party?"

"You mean Talbot didn't tell you himself?"

"He wouldn't say a word."

Max beamed. "What a decent specimen. My opinion of him grows and grows."

Having clipped the tags off Laura's new clothes, Ho held

them up. "We have here a pair of tan pleated chino slacks, a navy-and-tan striped T-shirt, and a navy jacket of which, I am told, you are to push up the sleeves. Here are espadrilles, woman's size nine and a half."

Laura pulled the T-shirt over her head. "It doesn't matter if you don't want to tell me about Theo Talbot, Max. I was just afraid at first it might be about Larry Todd."

"Oh, to have such a simple life as yours." Max sighed. "To answer your question: Talbot's and my imbroglio had nothing to do with Larry Todd or the Christmas party. Two years ago a lover's parents attempted to bring a morals charge against me. The Bellingham police were called in and Talbot was the officer in charge."

"The parents pressed a charge?"

"Tried. The boy was a student. The parents maintained I seduced the boy as a minor, although by the time I met him he was frightfully experienced. I blame the boy, actually; he was using me to shock his parents. Theo Talbot seemed disgusted with the whole thing but carried out his duties nonetheless. It eventually blew over, but not without leaving me an emotional wreck. I was on Valium until Ho made me quit." He looked dolefully at Ho. "Not a day goes by that I don't think about my lovely Valium."

"Metaphors do not come in bottles, Maximilian. You must seek them out yourself."

CHAPTER 13

Barbara Todd's swaybacked mare walked across the pasture for a handout. Laura first ignored the horse's snorts, then pulled up a hank of high grass to keep her quiet. Petting the mare, she surveyed the front pasture, gravel drive, and two-story frame house. Larry used to call this place "the farm," but the fact was the whole three acres was bog. Giving the mare one last pat, Laura walked up the drive and knocked on the door. Inside someone stirred.

The door was opened by an unkempt Barbara Todd. The widow was wearing gray sweats and brown leather oxfords and her hair was pulled into a ponytail. The streak in her hair ran like a scar from her forehead straight back to the rubber band. Her eyes didn't recognize Laura, only taking in the trendy clothes.

Laura began, "I'm sorry to bother you. I used to be a student of your hus—"

Barbara laughed. "I thought you were a boy."

"It's these clothes, isn't it? They really aren't very girly. May I come in?'

Barbara looked at her curiously. "Sure."

Leading Laura into the sun-filled living room, Barbara motioned toward a rattan sofa. For herself she chose a high-backed rocker flanked by a knitting stand and lamp. "What is it you've come about?"

"I don't know if you remember me; I did my master's under Larry on the dig at Keena."

"Laura Ireland, I thought it was you." Barbara curled her feet up under her and made the chair rock. Her voice had the edge of a buzz saw: "Did you cut your hair so I wouldn't recognize you? Were you too embarrassed?"

"Not embarrassed, more like reluctant."

"And you need something from me. Wait, I know what you want: It's your letters, isn't it? God, the irony." Barbara rocked the chair, smiling softly.

"My letters are here?"

"Of course they're here. You don't think we'd let garbage like that float around. Terrence Buchanan had the decency to bring them over as soon as we heard about Larry."

Laura stood up, "Where—" She sat down again: "Have you decided what to do with them?"

"Well, I don't know." Barbara leaned forward fiercely to rock the chair, "I haven't finished reading them yet; they're all so interesting. And I've yet to straighten out all the players, there are so many of you."

"I could—"

"Needn't to worry, I'll figure it out. Tell me, are you the one who cries when she thinks about the folk-urban continuum or the one who said she rode her bike out and spied on the house?"

"What?"

"Then maybe you're the one who gave him the watch."

"No watch. You mean somebody gave him that?"

"Oh, she's shocked. Come now, I thought you knew Larry. You really need to hear more of this, child, it's quite an education."

Barbara went into the den and came back with an unruly

packet of odd-sized and multicolored envelopes. Holding aloft
a sheet of blue paper she read: " 'Dear Larry, Images of your
expression in class keep me from concentrating on Wissler.
I constantly rehearse what I should have said when you asked
about culture areas—' "

"I didn't write that," said Laura.

Barbara kept reading. " 'Did my dull-wittedness disappoint you? I know you require an intellectual partner as well
as a sexual one and I hope one day I can be as good at the
former as the ladder.' L-a-d-d-e-r, 'ladder.' Gwen wrote that.
Oh yes, I remember Gwen." Barbara neatly refolded the letter. " 'Intellectual partner,' what a panic. Larry had a great
big intellect, didn't he?"

Laura didn't answer.

Barbara picked up a small yellow sheet: " 'Dear Larry,
I think of you lying in bed'—that's exactly what he did, lie
in bed—'I think of you lying in bed beside a woman you
cannot love and I ache all over with longing and pain. At
night, I pretend . . .' " Barbara flipped through, "Blah, blah,
very boring. All that longing and pain was brought to us from
'Love with my whole heart, Andrea.' Poor Andrea, do you
know her?"

"No."

Laura glanced at the pile in Barbara's lap. She couldn't
see any of her cream-colored stationery. Barbara continued
her sour reading, running through a Beverly who "loved
freely" and a Susan who knew unquestionably that "Larry
was the most important influence in her life after Buddhism."
After a while Barbara looked up and saw she had lost Laura's
interest. "I'm not being very helpful, am I? Which ones are
yours?" She fanned out the letters on her lap.

"I don't think mine are there."

"What do they look like?"

"Ivory stationery with deckle edges. I don't see any."

Barbara skimmed the packet. "Neither do I. Too bad. We
could have read some to see if you still feel the same about
Larry. Well, maybe we can just talk instead, girl talk." She
put the letters aside and rocked the chair. "For instance, I'm
dying to know if you enjoyed yourself with Larry."

"I don't think I should stay any longer."

"Sit down, dear girl. I'm perfectly willing to help you find your letters but first you're going to tell me about Larry. Now, when I say, 'Did you enjoy yourself with Larry?' I mean"—she raised her eyebrows—"Did you 'enjoy yourself.' "

Laura sat down and looked toward the door of the den. She knew the game Barbara was playing: back when Laura had played high school basketball they called it "Nervier Than Thou." It was a locker room psyche-out game and the black girls from East L.A. had been masters at it. But even in high school they played more elegantly than Barbara.

"Actually," Laura began, "I guess you couldn't say I enjoyed myself with Larry the way you mean." She shifted positions to get cozy. "When Larry and I slept together I was too nervous to orgasm, maybe too young. Anyway, a while back I read this book that says women have to take control of their own orgasms. I forget the title, but the author says women always expect men to know so much they end up surrendering control of their own bodies. It sounds like a good thesis to me, but sometime—"

"Be quiet."

"I'm not finished. I was going to explain what was wrong with making love with Larry. Now, maybe you had better luck with him than I, but looking back I think the real problem was that Larry was selfish and it made him a rotten lover. For instance, besides not caring whether I orgasmed or not, he used to make fun of my flat chest even though he knew I was sensitive about it. He said it looked like something a rabbit would suck on." Barbara put her hand to her mouth, trying to shut Laura's. Laura finished up, "Anyway I guess the bottom line is that I'm glad he was your problem and not mine."

Barbara sat stonily in the rocker; Laura checked her fingernails. The phone rang and Barbara jumped up and ran out to the kitchen. Laura, too, leapt up and went in the den. Larry's desk chair was pushed in, that wasn't a good sign. She pulled it out and looked under the desk; as she expected, there was no duffel.

Oak filing cabinets lined the opposite wall and Laura began opening and closing each drawer, just in case her letters were there. They weren't, and Barbara still chatted on the phone back in the kitchen.

The desk drawers were the last place to look, and with a heavy heart, Laura opened them all, expecting nothing, finding nothing either. She could hear Barbara making the last curt phone noises before good-bye, so she hurried back to the living room and sat down. She seated herself just in time to hear Barbara say, "I'll see what I can do. Good-bye."

Barbara came back and Laura stood up. "I'm going now, I don't—"

"No, you can't leave. Laura. Let me make you some coffee. I can help you. We'll talk about your letters. Please excuse my behavior. I have all this unchanneled anger and I'm directing it in the wrong places. it would really be good therapy for me to help you."

"Where do *you* think my letters are?"

Barbara walked toward the kitchen, motioning for Laura to follow. "That's an interesting question when you're dealing with someone like Larry. He could be awfully devious sometimes. Are you married? Of course not." She poured old coffee into the sink and rinsed the glass pot under the tap. "Let me give you some advice. Don't ever equate handsome with good—that's the mistake. Even Larry's mother knew he was devious. She said that by the age of nine Larry had figured out how to con people with his choir boy routine. He'd just smile and break their hearts. Nine. Can you believe it? The only reason he got away with it for so long was his raw IQ points; he was just plain smart."

"I know."

"I have a degree in anthropology too," added Barbara.

"Barbara, I have a question."

"Anything. Yes?"

"Do you know where Larry's duffel bag is?"

"No, I haven't seen it lately." Barbara's eyes became distant. "Come to think of it, he'd been picking up some nice things lately; it might be worth something. Don't get excited, the duffel doesn't belong to you; I've read the will, it belongs to me. Oh, I see; you think your letters are in it. Now why do you think that, were you his special one?"

"It doesn't seem now like anybody was his special one,

does it? My letters might be there because I can't find them anyplace else.''

"Now where is his duffel? Maybe I should call Terrence.''

"Dr. Buchanan doesn't know anything about it. He didn't even believe me the other day when I told him Larry sold artifacts.''

"Don't kid yourself; you'd be surprised how much a chairman knows.''

Laura heard crunching on the gravel drive and looked out to see a sky-blue police car pass the window. Barbara shrieked, "They're here!" She dropped the glass pot in the sink, breaking it to shards. Running to the front door, she yelled, "Hurry, she's in the kitchen, I can't keep her much longer.''

Laura started to unchain the kitchen door but by the time she had it open, two uniformed officers were strutting on the stoop. She ran to the front door and found Barbara blocking the threshold triumphantly. "They called and asked me to catch you. You're wanted by the police.'' She shouted outside. "Hurry, she's trying to get away!''

On the drive Theo Talbot climbed out of a patrol car still wearing his chamois shirt and chinos. He looked at Laura and they both froze in their tracks. His eyes told Laura how strange she looked with cropped hair and men's clothes. She turned and ran upstairs.

Barbara called, "Don't let her jump out the window!''

Upstairs Laura opened the door to a closet. Larry's camping junk was inside. She closed it and looked around. There were no locks on doors, no place to hide, except the bathroom. Down through the stair railings she saw Theo climbing up, the two patrolmen behind him. Laura darted to the bathroom and twisted the skeleton bolt. She stood motionless, holding her breath and listening.

In a few seconds there was movement on the other side of the door, then a gentle rap. "Laura, open the door. I want to talk to you.''

"Like last night when you chained me to the bed?'

"That part's over now. A lot of people are out here and if you don't open the door, we have to open it ourselves.''

"I hope you rot in hell.''

"Don't talk like that. And don't threaten anything, either; we have to take you at your word. If you don't open the door we have to charge you with resisting arrest. Please listen, it's serious this time."

"You listen to me, Theo Talbot. I haven't done anything wrong and if I opened the door I know you won't let me go back to Seattle, would you?"

"Open up and we can talk about it."

"Sure we can."

"I've got a lot to tell you. Did you know you were exactly right about Jimmy Patterson not killing Adele? He sat in a Dutch Harbor tavern all day Saturday. Checks out clean, lots of witnesses."

"Big deal. You're entirely missing a guy named Barry Cunliffe who came up to Keena this morning. I bet you didn't even know he's one of Larry's old graduate students."

"Barry's harmless."

"How do you know? He could very easily have been in with Larry on the smuggling."

"Barry heard I was up in Keena and came up to be my guide. He didn't know I had such a competent female interpreter with me."

"Good try, Talbot, why don't you use some of your other macho tricks? I know you have plenty."

"Damn it, Laura, that hurts."

"Good."

Laura went to the window and pushed back the lace curtain. Barbara's mare was down by the fence grazing peacefully and the police car blocked the drive. The window itself was high and small and jutted out in a dormer. On both sides of the dormer the shingle roof fell steeply away. She heard murmuring through the door and then the word "hinges." She looked with alarm, then relief, seeing the hinges were on her side.

From the other side of the door someone started tinkering with the old-fashioned skeleton lock. Laura snatched a tube of toothpaste and squeezed it into the keyhole. A voice said, "Jesus Christ," and she stopped squeezing. Out in the hall someone laughed. She crossed again to the window and knelt on the clothes hamper for a better view outside. Below the window there was enough sloping roof to stand on. If she stood on the hamper she could climb out.

"Laura, I'm going to ask you seriously and then start taking action, do you hear me?"

Laura said nothing.

"At least talk to me."

She contemplated the weighted sash, wondering how much noise it would make. "What do you want me to say? Say I'm sorry I wouldn't stay chained to your bed?"

"Are you ready?"

"No, I'm not ready. Just a minute." She flushed the toilet, using the sound to cover the window opening.

"Okay, ready? Here's your last chance. Open this door by order of the Bellingham Police. Do it, Laura, I'm not kidding this time."

She climbed out on to the roof.

"Okay, we're calling a fire truck to take the door off. And when we come in don't try to fight or use anything for a weapon. Are you listening?"

Laura quietly closed the sash. Crouching on the roof, she looked at the ground fifteen feet blow. Nearby was a thicket of snowberry bushes—if she dared jump. She processed the idea, but couldn't remember if high falls broke the metatarsals in the feet or the ankle bones in the lower leg. "Wimp," she whispered.

Directly below her someone opened the front door. Scurrying up the roof, she lay down on the other side of the ridgeline. From the car out front came the sound of the officer joining in the radio chatter. He went back inside closing the door behind him. Laura tiptoed over the roof crest and stared at the patch of snowberry bushes again. She just couldn't do it.

A minute later she heard radio chatter far down the road, then the roar of a fire truck's diesel engine. The truck would arrive in less than a minute. Taking off her spiffy new jacket, she dropped it into the bushes. Tiptoeing over the roof crest, she lay down again.

The fire truck stormed the driveway and braked behind the squad car. Through the roof Laura heard the firemen enter the house and pound up the stairs in their heavy boots. Next she heard an electric drill: They were removing the bathroom lock. The drilling stopped. She heard Theo's muffled voice, "Laura, don't do anything dumb, okay?"

In a moment the window sash banged and a voice said to the great outdoors, "She jumped." One by one heads were thrust out the window, given to agitated cursing, then drawn back inside. ". . . the jacket . . . don't touch . . . the dog." Laura listened with her whole body. She heard the troop pounding down the stairs.

In a few minutes Laura peeked over the roofline again. No one was in the yard. She climbed back in the open window, walked through the bathroom, and listened at the top of the stairs. ". . . for the dog."

Laura's heart began to hammer and she fought a rising panic. Tiptoeing to the hall closet she went in and closed the door behind her. The closet smelled of Larry, and of camping in Keena. She dropped to the floor and covered herself with his sleeping bag. Pulling his L.L. Bean field boots from under her bottom, she set them by the crack under the door. Holding her breath, she sat waiting for the dog to come and end the game.

Laura sat very still. She could hear nothing under her stifling tent and she didn't dare get up. In a while she heard faint barking from down in the yard. Pulling up the sleeping bag, she listened to the dog's bark and the frantic neighing of the mare. Someone cursed. Men shouted directions to one another in loud strained voices. Laura covered herself again. She sat hugging her knees, quietly breathing the heavy unwashed scent of the late Larry Todd. She sat there for five hours.

When Laura took the sleeping bag off there was no light under the closet door. She listened a moment, then opened the knob. Darkness had fallen. The only light was from a streetlamp out on the road. Down in the kitchen Barbara Todd was running water. It was time to make an exit out the front door.

Laura tiptoed down the stairs. Suddenly a car turned into the drive and the stairwell was filled with the yellow light.

She ran up to the hall closet again and stood inside, leaving the door ajar.

The caller was a male, a genial baritone. She recognized the voice of Bushman's father, Dr. Buchanan. "A sympathy call," Laura murmured. "Ever the gentleman."

She could hear Barbara too, laughing and talking with lots of animation. *Good for her, she needs to loosen up.* Laura listened as they chatted, Barbara obviously enjoying Dr. Buchanan's rich baritone humor. Laura hoped it was a short visit and that Buchanan wouldn't be too terribly brilliant. After ten minutes the conversation dropped in volume: the signal Buchanan was leaving.

Opening the door, Laura was hit with a sight as shocking as the water of Keena Inlet: The stairwell light flashed on and Barbara and Dr. Buchanan climbed toward her. Buchanan's hand was on Barbara's fanny as she walked a few stairs ahead of him. Buchanan was pleading a case, "I know what he's put you through but that doesn't solve my immediate problem. Where else could I hire as cheap and nasty?"

"Nasty, certainly."

"Perhaps her morals are amiss but I've already called to check, and her adviser says she's doing first-rate work. I wouldn't do it without your permission, however."

They walked past the closet into the bedroom and shut the door behind them.

Laura slipped down the stairs and out the front door. Breaking into a loose jog on the driveway, she scanned the fields for the antique mare. *Just as well not to find her,* Laura thought: *Now isn't the time to get caught for stealing a horse.* She ran the four miles into town.

CHAPTER 14

A police car was parked down on the street in front of Endicott House and upstairs at Ho's the lights were on. Laura climbed the neighbor's front steps and pushed through the hedge to the rose garden. Up in Ho's bay window a uniformed cop stood gesturing to unseen listeners.

Laura took the rockery steps up to the back alley and tiptoed across the wooden gangplank to the kitchen door. Slumping down on her bottom, she let out a sigh and muttered, "Deep doo-doo." How had she gotten into this much trouble? All she wanted were her letters to Larry.

The alley was suddenly illuminated by car lamps. Laura scrambled out of the light and slid underneath the wooden rail to the damp ground five feet below the porch. Stumbling up to the side of the house, she pressed herself against it. A spiderweb clung to her face and nail heads in the planking above scratched her scalp. The car pulled up to Endicott House and parked, leaving its motor running. Laura held her breath and stood motionless against the house. Footsteps sounded on the gangplank.

There was a knock on the door and from inside she heard movement. The door opened and Ho Kauffmann blurted to the visitor, "Did you find her?"

Directly above her head, Theo answered. "I guess that means she hasn't shown up here either. May I use the phone?" He walked in and the door closed behind him. Laura listened to the murmuring in the kitchen, her heart pounding in her throat. If she went up and turned herself in, she would probably end up spending the night in jail. And how would that look on her résumé?

In a moment the door opened and Theo walked out on the porch again. From the kitchen an unknown male voice spoke to him in low tones: "I tend to think Kauffmann's for real. Her suitcase is still here. You got somebody waiting down in Seattle?"

"A suit is sitting in her hotel hallway."

"Where are you going now?"

Theo answered, "The trailer. As far as I can tell she's still looking for her love letters, and the one place she hasn't looked is inside the trailer."

Laura bit her lip. Above her head Theo walked across the gangplank to the alley. From the door, the other officer called, "How long do I stay here?"

"The whole shift if you have to. She'll show up." The car door slammed and Theo drove away. The kitchen light went out and Laura climbed up the low retaining wall into the alley. She looked into Ho's lighted dining-room windows and wondered what to do.

A hundred feet up the alley a shadowed man strolled toward her. His head was down and his hands were stuffed in the pockets of his tweed battle jacket. As he turned into the condo parking garage across from Ho's, he stopped in his tracks.

"Miss Ireland, is that you?"

"Dean Siecetti! Do you live here?"

He smiled sweetly. "Last time I looked. I believe you've

cut your hair since yesterday.'' His lilting foreign voice was
a balm.

Laura nodded, her voice breaking as she spoke. ''I'm
really glad to see you.''

''Miss Ireland, what's wrong? Has this Todd business es-
calated?''

''I'll say it has.'' She glanced at Ho's windows. ''Is there
someplace we can talk?''

''Certainly.'' He gestured to the lighted condo garage.
''I'm on the third floor. Won't you come up?'' Laura quickly
walked in.

Beyond the garage, a lighted corridor snaked past storage
closets and a laundry room. Beyond the laundry room a sign
on the wall pointed to the elevator. Siecetti took out a key
and inserted it into the elevator panel, and as they waited
Laura looked down at the dean's Gucci loafers and cuffed
wool trousers. Her own boyish cottons seemed pedestrian in
contrast.

Self-consciously, Siecetti and Laura rode the mirrored
brass elevator up to the third floor, where they got out into a
hallway of ankle-deep dusty rose carpet. On the wall were
bold abstract prints in rose, teal, and gray. ''Please forgive
the decorating,'' Siecetti said. ''It's been done professionally.''

Laura blinked. ''I think it's nice.''

''Dates itself rather quickly, I think.'' He escorted her to
the last of the three doors on the hall and opened it. As he
turned on the lights behind her, Laura cried, ''Ekkkk.''

Across the entry hall was a tall, freestanding, three-sided
mirror. It had undulating sides and a rounded top that made
reflections look strangely organic. Laura walked over to examine it. The mirror was more like sculpture than decora-
tion.

''I'm so sorry you were startled,'' Siecetti said. ''It was
a gift from a friend in Venice and I've no other place to put
it at the moment.''

As Siecetti hung his coat Laura looked around the entry
hall. Tan and gold Persian rugs covered a floor of wide
bleached oak planks. On the reedy grasscloth wall hung a
small Picasso cartoon for *Guernica*: the horse with its mouth

upturned in pain. As she entered the living room the view of the bay and lighted city enticed her across the room. Siecetti's far wall was entirely of glass, and beyond his balcony the city twinkled like Christmas against the midnight blackness of the water.

Turning back to look at the room, she saw that the remaining walls were alternately blond hardwood or textured grasscloth. Laid over the oak floorboards were glowing russet Persians spread so thickly they overlapped. On the wall above the couch was a strangely malevolent painting of a carnival scene. Old-lady children rode the merry-go-round under violet skies while orange-faced adults looked on. All the other walls were covered with twentieth-century paintings, some by the same violet-and-orange artist.

"This is a beautiful apartment," Laura said.

"Thank you. I enjoy it very much. May I get you something to drink—beer, wine, cola?"

"Coke would be fine. Actually, if you have some leftovers, I haven't had dinner yet."

"Dear girl. Come with me." Siecetti turned on his heel and walked to the kitchen.

The kitchen was as highly styled as the rest of the house. The restaurant-sized stove had a hammered-metal exhaust hood and the many spigots at the tiled sink were polished brass. The walls were earthy glazed tile and the floors were bleached hardrock maple, polished as smooth as a squash court. Siecetti pulled out a maple stool for Laura and gestured for her to sit down. Opening the refrigerator door, he spoke into the lighted box: "I have leftover salmon, cold stuffed mushrooms, one more serving of spaghetti, and some Genoa salami."

"Yes, anything will be fine."

"Spaghetti in the microwave? A salami sandwich?"

"What about the spaghetti first and then a sandwich?" Laura repositioned herself on the stool, relaxing a little now that someone had addressed her hunger. "Thank you for taking me in like this, I find I'm a bit of an embarrassment to my friends right now."

As Siecetti scraped spaghetti and sauce onto a plate, he glanced up. "You must tell me what you've done."

"I ran away from the police."

"Do you have something they want? The artifacts, perhaps?"

"No, nothing like that. Actually, I can't help them at all. Detective Talbot just seems to be picking on me."

Siecetti smiled and his amber eyes glowed merrily. "Perhaps he has his own reasons."

Watching as he punched in two minutes on the microwave timer, Laura said, "If he does, then it's called harassment." She stared at the dancing digits as they measured the time in which her food would be ready. When given her steaming plate, Laura immediately cut the spaghetti into two-inch lengths so she could wolf it down more quickly. As she ate, Dean Siecetti made her a sandwich.

When she finished the spaghetti, the dean set a sandwich before her and poured a glass of milk. As she ate he watched anxiously from a kitchen stool, anticipating her need for a napkin and a second glass of milk. When she had finished he asked solicitously, "Would you like coffee?"

Laura wiped her mouth. "No, thank you."

"Tea? Cocoa?"

"No, thank you. I really don't want to be a bother."

"It's no bother, really." He put his hand on an arching brass spigot at the side of the sink. "This tap dispenses boiling water. I can make a cup of something hot with no trouble at all."

"Well, in that case a cup of cocoa would be very nice."

"Good." Siecetti went to the oak cabinet and took out a cocoa packet. As he poured the contents into a cup and filled it from the steaming spigot, he said, "Every time I use this spigot I think about the high contrast between the luxuries we are all so used to and the extreme hardships of others. I hadn't realized until all this business with Todd that there are actually people in this very county who had no running water."

Laura lifted her chin. "You've been to the trailer?"

Siecetti stared, and shock widened his heavy-lidded eyes. "I hate to admit it, but I'm a bit of a sensationalist. I told myself I needed to go there in order to see the place where one of my faculty was killed. I hope you don't find that repelling?''

Laura shook her head. "Not at all. I'm still fascinated by fires.''

As she sipped her cocoa he asked, "Now, Miss Ireland, what can I do to be of help?''

"Gee, that's nice of you to ask.''

Siecetti shrugged. "My job often entails helping people. In fact, in a lot of ways a dean is something of a doormat.''

"I don't want to be any trouble.''

"Be trouble, go ahead. I'm used to it.''

Laura shifted on her stool. "Well, the single most useful thing you could do would be to help me find the letters I wrote to Larry Todd when I was in graduate school.''

Siecetti nodded. "I hear you've been making quite a fuss over them.''

"I guess I have.''

"I would love to help you find them, dear, but if a young resourceful person like yourself has had no luck, I seriously doubt I would do any better.''

"Oh.'' Laura's face fell. "Well then, the other thing I could use is help with getting the Bellingham police not to prosecute, or whatever it is they want to do to me.''

"Again, I'm afraid I can't help you. I must tell you outright that I disagree with your tactics. The way always to deal with the police is to face them head-on.''

Laura looked down at her cocoa.

"I've disappointed you, haven't I? To you I'm just a silly, useless old man.''

"No, not at all.'' Laura avoided his eyes.

"Yes I am. I can see it in your face.'' Siecetti drummed his fingers and looked around the kitchen. "That cocoa certainly looks good. Do you mind if I make a cup and join you.''

"Of course not.''

Siecetti went to the cabinet. Laura watched as he poured cocoa into a cup and turned on the boiling-water tap. The stream of bubbling water flowed from the arching spigot like liquid silver. Laura leaped off the stool and cried, "The water heater!''

"I beg your pardon?"

"The Tsamian artifacts are in Adele Patterson's water heater. It's not connected to anything and the inner tank was lying in a garbage dump near the trailer. Adele took it out, or got somebody else to take it out. We've got to go see."

Siecetti put down his cup, hands trembling. "Are you sure?"

"No, but where else can they be? And my letters! My letters must be there, too."

"How wonderful for you. We must go immediately."

Laura sat down. "We can't. Theo Talbot is out there waiting for me."

"He is?"

She nodded. "I heard him tell another policeman he was going out there because I might show up to look for my letters."

"He was right then, wasn't he?"

"What am I going to do?"

"You really are in a mess, aren't you?" He poured his untouched cocoa into the sink and came over to clean up after Laura. Laura walked to the window and looked down at the bay. "If I had my letters back, I don't think I would even care what the police did to me."

"But surely Detective Talbot won't let you take them from under his nose."

"But surely."

Siecetti raised his hands to his chest. "I can go."

"What? I don't see how you would do any better than I would. Talbot can be awfully stubborn."

Siecetti shrugged. "I can be a most persuasive man. You forget that my job requires me to deal with academics, some of the most creatively stubborn people ever born." He smiled and his amber eyes glowed.

Laura laughed a clear chiming note. The sound surprised her and she laughed again. It was the first time she had relaxed in days. "Would you really go, Dean Siecetti?"

"Of course I would go. It hurts my pride to be thought of as a silly, useless old man."

"Should I wait here for you?"

Siecetti got up. "A very good idea. You can make yourself at home: beverages, food, there are books and magazines in the living room.''

''Super.'' Laura got up and followed him down the hall. In the living room Siecetti said, ''Won't you make yourself comfortable here? I need to change clothes if I'm to go out to the great woods.'' He went into the bedroom and closed the door.

Laura walked around the room peering at the paintings and then settled herself on the sofa with a magazine. In a few minutes Siecetti came out wearing khaki field trousers and carrying a long canvas gun case.

Laura looked up. ''What's that for?'' she asked.

Smiling sheepishly, Siecetti held up the gun case. ''I must confess that I'm not the typical American woodsman. The forest panics me.''

''You really shouldn't worry: Theo Talbot carries a pistol under his coat.''

Siecetti held the case up higher. ''I like this much better. It's big, and it's loud. Will you be all right here?''

''Yes, I'm quite comfortable.''

''If you get tired, you can go to sleep on the sofa. Just take a pillow and blanket from the bed.''

''Thank you. I really appreciate this. This is the first time I've felt like this might work out all right.''

''And it will.'' He left the apartment.

Laura picked up her magazine again and flipped through the pages. Letting out a luxurious sigh, she kicked off her shoes and put her feet up on upholstery. Being in Siecetti's apartment felt like sitting in the waiting room of a very expensive physician: don't worry, Doctor will take care of everything.

After she had finished the magazine, she got up and went to the other side of the room to open the door of an antique armoire. Inside the cabinet was Video City: television, VCR, radio, amplifier, tape deck, CD player, and stereo turntable. The CDs were mostly opera and chamber music. The stereo records were Big Band from the forties. Laura turned on the TV and settled down to wait for the Seattle news at ten.

Yawning her way through the news, she perked up when they came to sports. As expected, there was a fleeting fifteen seconds devoted to the volleyball tournament with an obligatory shot of Tom Selleck spiking. Women's results were not reported. Turning off the TV, Laura went into the bedroom for a blanket and pillow.

The bedroom was carpeted in deep beige wool. The bed was oversized, covered in quilted slubbed silk, and mounted on a carpeted dais. Laura took a pillow, but couldn't bring herself to disturb the sumptious bedspread. As she passed the dresser a beautiful brass-and-leather dresser tray caught her eye. Peeking in, she saw pennies, keys, a restaurant receipt, and a familiar-looking carved ivory dolphin.

Without thinking, Laura picked up the delightful little dolphin. The animal had a merry closemouthed smile and finely carved flukes. It was identical to the one on the end of the Tsamian Dolphin Ladle. Turning it on end, she saw that the tip of the tail was rough where it had been snapped off its support. Fingering the smooth little carving, she tried desperately to understand why Dean Siecetti might have the Tsamian dolphin.

Suddenly chill bumps began at the back of her neck and ran down her arms: if Dean Siecetti had the dolphin, he must have stolen it. No, Larry must have stolen it and given it to the dean. Her mind would not work fast enough. She formed the picture of the dean walking out with his gun case. As she looked in the mirror, her heart pounded so hard she could feel it against her ribs: the dean—who wanted Tsamian artifacts—was taking a gun to the trailer where Theo Talbot waited.

The pillow dropped from under her arm and Laura bolted from the room. Out in the hall she found that the elevator panel worked only with a key. She raced to the stairs and bounded down three flights so fast she was dizzy at the bottom. Sprinting out the basement corridor through the garage, she spanned Ho's gangplank in three steps and pounded on his backdoor. "Ho, open the door. Hurry, it's an emergency!" She beat on the door until the windows rattled.

In the kitchen the light went on and Ho looked at her through the panes of glass. Opening the door, he said, "Laura! You're safe. The police just left here."

"Call them back. Theo Talbot's in trouble." Laura pushed

past him and took the Honda keys off the wall. "Tell them to go to Adele Patterson's trailer as fast as they can. Dean Siecetti is going to kill him."

"What?"

"I'm not kidding."

"Laura, there's no—"

"I'm not kidding." She ran out the door. "Call the police." She unlocked the car door and explained frantically, "Dean Siecetti has a tiny Tsamian sculpture. I recognized it from the museum." Climbing in the car, she rolled down the window. "He brought a rifle to the trailer." Backing into the alley, she shouted out the window. "Stop looking at me and *do* something." She sped down the alley.

CHAPTER 15

Laura drove east through the moonlit country. Above the foothills stood ghostly Mount Baker, drawing her—as if by gravity—to its snowy mass. Jamming her foot to the floor, she sped past lush fields on the Nooksack floodplain and through barbed-wire intersections where Holsteins had gathered for the night. At each intersection and each gravel parking lot, she honked hard on the horn, hoping to attract one of the famous sheriff's deputies Darby had praised so highly.

Halfway to the trailer the rich floodplain gave way to hummocky scrub growth and hard-luck farms. After a few more miles the farming landscape changed entirely to logging. Laura honked as she passed the Bull of the Woods Tavern and the Deming Grange. Noisily, she blew her horn past the parking lot at the shingle mill with its mountains of sawdust and defunct tepee burner.

Twenty miles down the Mount Baker Highway—still having attracted no cop—she turned onto the Soule Road. Three miles down the Soule, she turned into a dirt driveway she hoped was Adele's. Turning off the headlights, she drove slowly in the dark. Potholes jounced her nearly to the roof.

A quarter mile down the drive she came to the garbage-dump clearing. Pulling the car off to the side, she got out and quietly shut the door. In the moonlight the dump looked luminous and wonderful. The shadowy Chevrolet shone like a monument to technology and the glowing enamel appliances looked usable and clean.

Laura walked up the road listening for sounds. The moist woods smelled of night, and damp earth cushioned her steps. Trying her best to avoid brittle twigs and leaves, she trod in the worn tire ruts as wet ferns brushed against her cotton pants. She had no idea what she would do when she got to the trailer.

Several hundred yards down the drive she saw a small light in the middle of the road. Creeping forward, she found a large dark sedan with its trunk open. A small bulb illuminated the inside, and in the dim light Laura saw Siecetti's empty gun case. A whimper came out of her mouth and she bit the back of her hand to silence herself: Theo was in trouble, perhaps even dead. It was her fault.

Far down the road she saw a square of light from the trailer window. Padding around the bulky sedan, she brushed past the hood and knocked off one several newspaper-wrapped objects piled on it. She picked up the bundle and brought it back to the lighted trunk. Unwrapping, she found a shaman's mask—Tsamian or Bella Coola—with pursed whistling lips and narrow eye slits.

Setting the mask in the trunk, she went back to look at the other bundles on the hood. In the faint light she unwrapped one and found a shallow carved bowl, the kind the Timpkish made for the Vancouver museum shop. Unwrapping a bigger bundle, she pulled out a oversized ceremonial rattle. She held it up in the moonlight and saw that the rattle was a life-sized horned owl. It was as heavy as a medicine ball and the handle as thick as baseball bat. Grabbing the handle, she found she could barely manage it with one hand.

She shook it and pebbles rolled around inside. Satisfied with her weapon, she trudged toward the trailer.

Close to the trailer, Laura crouched down to look. A police car was pulled up almost to the redwood fencing that hid the garbage cans from view. The light in the kitchen was on and people passed back and forth in front of the window. Laura tiptoed close and walked quietly around the fencing to the far back window and peered in. Theo stood by the cabinet holding newspaper bundles and Siecetti stood in front of the window with his back toward her. From this vantage point she could hear the rhythms of Siecetti's low sweet voice but could not understand what he said. Holding her rattle down to keep the pebbles quiet, she padded around to the short side of the trailer and crouched underneath the dinette windows to listen. The garbage cans smelled of rotting food.

All of a sudden the door slammed opened. Laura froze against the aluminum siding. Theo walked down the steps and past the patrol car carrying some newspaper bundles. Behind him came Siecetti, pointing a double-barreled gun at Theo's back. The men marched silently down the drive and disappeared in the dark. Laura stood up and looked in the window. On the dinette table was the blue metal lid to the water heater and beside it several more wrapped parcels. Laura moved over behind the redwood fencing and nestled beside the garbage cans, resting the owl rattle on the ground.

In a minute Theo and Siecetti returned. Siecetti was speaking in low tones and she held her breath to listen. " . . . can kill you now or later, it makes no difference to me." They shuffled up the steps and closed the door. Again Laura darted over to the windows. Again she could hear only murmurs through the wall. This time Siecetti was very angry.

The door opened suddenly and Siecetti lectured, " . . . stupid mouth. You wouldn't have even tried if you understood who you're dealing with. We both know I won't be caught, and the reason is that I am not a killer by nature and they have no reason to suspect me."

As they walked down the stairs Laura shifted again to her spot by the garbage cans so she would not be seen.

"Not there!" Siecetti commanded. Laura froze. "This way, Mr. Talbot. You're becoming too recalcitrant. This time we're going to the latrine. How long do you think it would take them to find a body down there?''

They walked past the opening between the trailer and the fencing. Laura held stone still and Siecetti continued, "You disappoint me, Mr. Talbot. I was waiting for a scatological remark.''

"Guess I'm not the outdoor type."

"Stop! Stop right there!" Siecetti was furious.

Holding her breath, Laura waited. The men stood directly on the other side of the fence from her. Crouching against the trash cans, she barely dared to blink.

Siecetti snarled, "Did you think by making footprints you could leave a trail? That's too stupid for words. I want you to bend over slowly and take off your shoes. Slower! Slower than that! You mustn't excite me, you know, it's very dangerous to your health.''

Laura peeked around the side of the fence. Siecetti stood with his back toward her, training his twin barrels on Theo, who crouched before him. Theo had taken off one shoe and was shifting feet to untie the other.

Laura pulled her head back around the fence and clutched her rattle tightly.

In a few seconds Siecetti snapped again, "No! Don't pick up your shoes. I'll dispose of them later. Go on, get walking. What are you waiting for?''

Silence followed.

"Well?" purred Siecetti.

Without thinking, Laura stood up and grabbed the top of the fence with her left hand. Leaping off the ground from a standing takeoff, she braced herself on the top of the rail with her left arm and swung the heavy rattle around in her right. At the last second Siecetti saw her with the rattle and slightly shifted left, still training his gun on Theo.

Raising the rattle over her head, Laura directed her gaze on the spot he had come from, but aimed her blow squarely for the top of his moving head. The rattle landed with a sickening thud. The owl rattle dropped out of her hand and clattered off the hood of the patrol car, pebbles shaking as it rolled.

Laura watched in horror as Siecetti shook off the blow, never once taking his gun sites off Theo.

"Run, Laura!" Theo shouted.

Laura didn't move, afraid if she ran she'd get shot in back. In the yellow glow from the kitchen she could see a soft glazed expression on Siecetti's face. He stared glassy-eyed at Theo as Theo waited, frozen to the spot. Siecetti stared at his prey and a long second went by. Peering over the fence, Laura waited for Siecetti to shoot. Slowly the gun barrel began to waver. Then Siecetti turned up the corners of his mouth in a sweet stupid smile and, waiting a moment, dropped to his knees. Theo was on him in an instant.

Darting around the fence, Laura found Theo kneeling on Siecetti's back, twisting his arm up almost to his head. The long gleaming gun was beside them on the ground.

". . . arm," moaned Siecetti, his mouth smashed against wet earth.

Theo ignored him. "Laura, run down to Siecetti's car. In his trunk is my sport coat and my .thirty-eight. There are handcuffs in the coat pocket. I need them and the pistol. Quick."

Laura ran down the dark drive.

"Leave the safety on. Be careful," he called to her back.

A few minutes later, as she viewed the handcuffed prisoner in the caged backseat of the patrol car, Laura asked, "What if he tries to open the door with his feet?"

Theo reached inside the car to cradle the microphone in the console. "There aren't any door handles in the back of a patrol car, Laura." Craning his head inside toward Siecetti, he said, "She's going to bring you some ice for your head." Siecetti stared stonily at the steel mesh.

"Can't you come inside?" Laura asked.

"I'd better baby-sit out here. I called town instead of the sheriff's office and it's going to be a while before anybody shows up."

"Why'd you do that? The sheriff's closer."

"If you don't mind, I'd like to act like everything's been cool."

"Sure. I don't mind. It's partly my fault."

His dark eyes glowed in the light from the kitchen. "You know you just saved my life, don't you?"

Laura beamed. "I really did, didn't I?"

Theo took in the smile lines around her eyes sculpted by the soft yellow light. "Yeah, well, don't let it go to your head, okay?"

Laura laughed and walked up the trailer steps. Inside, the kitchen was worse than she remembered. Unwashed plates on the counter grew feathery mold and beside the toaster small rodents had taken up residence in a package of paper napkins. Laura opened the freezer door and found the ice trays empty. Calling back outside, she said, "No ice, Theo. Someone should really turn the electricity off, don't you think?"

Looking around the kitchen, she saw that Theo and Siecetti had only started unpacking the water heater. She went over to the table to look at a thin item wrapped in *Vancouver Sun*s. Tearing off the paper, she exposed an ivory ladle. Nearly a foot and a half long, it began in a deep flat-bottomed bowl and tapered to a sleekly elegant curving handle. Laura picked it up at both ends and held it to admire.

Just then Theo came up the steps and stood in the doorway. "What about Siecetti?" Laura asked.

"Keeled over on the seat. Out cold. What are you doing?"

She turned around so he could see the ladle. "This is the Dolphin Ladle. It was stolen from the museum. And look." She dipped into her pocket. "I found this at Siecetti's." Opening her hand, she held up the exquisite little dolphin, then placed it at the tip of the spoon. Theo smiled. "He looks like he's ready to leap off the spoon."

"He does, doesn't he?"

Theo took the dolphin and admired the laughing eyes and merry closemouthed smile. "I know that smile," he said. "It reminds me of somebody."

"*Mona Lisa.*"

"Exactly. You must be prescient."

"No. A lot of people have said that. This smile is actually a fairly typical facial feature in archaic and primitive sculpture. You see it a lot on Greek *kouri* and early Romanesque virgins.'' She held it again at the tip of the spoon. ''And see? A nineteenth-century Tsamian halfway around the world carved it on a dolphin.''

''Charms the pants off one.''

Glancing at the water heater, Laura said, ''Theo, can't we see what else is inside? I could identify some of it for you.''

Screwing up his face, he said, ''I suppose you could help inventory the stuff. But don't touch anything yet, I need to get some paper and some gloves from the trunk.''

Laura waited eagerly, peering into the shadowy enamel tank. When Theo came back, he carried a legal pad under his arm and two pairs of translucent latex gloves. Handing her a pair, he said, ''Here you go, champ.''

''Champ?''

As he pulled on his gloves he said. ''I talked to Claudia Buchanan earlier today. She said you were nationally ranked in volleyball.''

''Claudia's ranked, too. Only we call her Bushman.''

''You didn't tell me you were *that* good.''

''You didn't ask.''

From the water heater Laura pulled out a package the size of a small baseball bat. Ripping off the paper, she held up a flat-sided cedar salmon, carved all over with ovoid scales and Tsamian eyes. Above the tail was a handle-shaped area incised with deep cross-hatching.

''What's that thing?'' Theo asked.

''It's a fish club. You hold it here, just above the tail. It was used during the salmon runs in late summer when the men had to club a year's supply of fish to death. They used these clubs to turn the process into ritual slaughter; it makes the whole thing easier to bear. This belongs to somebody in Rebecca George's family.''

''Really? How can you tell?''

''The men in her family are famous carvers; they're in all the literature.'' She handed him the club. ''Their trademark is this extra indentation on the fish scales. See?''

Theo held the club out and moved it with minute motions of his wrist. ''Puts the old Louisville Slugger to shame. Is this from the museum?''

"Yes, I think so."

Dipping in again, Laura let out a cry. "Oh, this has been smashed." She quickly unwrapped a squashy bundle to expose dozens of flat little geometric carvings, brightly colored and feather-trimmed, like renegades from a patchwork quilt. "Thank heavens—frontlets, and they're not damaged."

"What are frontlets?"

"They go on the forehead—here—during ceremonies. This is enough for a whole clan."

They pulled out rattles, daggers, and several small masks, all carved with ovals and eyes and stained in Tsamian black, red, and white. Theo stopped to admire a particularly nice raven rattle on a handle. "This is like John's," he said and he turned it over to view the wings since John was not there to stop him. On the bird's back a tiny bug-eyed man obscenely stuck out his tongue; Theo turned the rattle over and put it down.

Peering inside the tank again, he asked, "What's that long bundle against the side?"

"Bring it out."

He bent over and pulled it out. "Oh no, it's broken. It's the beak off a mask."

Laura took it gently. "It's not broken. See these square bumps? They're tenons, they fit into mortise holes in the beak. It comes apart for storage. Oh, Theo, this is the snout from Tory's family's bear mask. We need to call her."

"I'm afraid the Georges can't have it for a while. It's evidence right now."

Theo held up the wooden bear snout. It was beautifully carved and had a gaping mouth set with hundreds of ivory teeth. Each tooth was a carved figure, detailed and individual. Everyone was there: old, young, female, male, happy, sad, animal, human. "How long do you suppose it takes to carve something like that?"

"It's not a question anyone would ask," Laura said.

"Look here. Here's a tooth that looks like you." He pointed out a thin female. "And here's me," he said, showing her a tall man. "Darn. Wouldn't you know it, I'm standing between an old woman and a dog."

"A play for sympathy, I can tell. How's Siecetti?"

Theo peered out the window. "Still laying down." He admired the bear teeth for a minute, then put the snout on the dinette table. Reaching deep into the tank, he pulled out a little clinking package. Laura snatched it away and unwrapped feverishly. "It's my bracelets. Theo, I found these at the dig. I wish I . . ."

"Could find your letters?"

"Yes. That's it. Look, this bracelet is my favorite."

She took out a thick cuff in the shape of a dwarf-legged man whose arms circled backward. His locked hands formed the clasp.

"That's hysterical," said Theo. "Is this funny to a Tsamian?"

"They'd probably say he was Bowkous, wild man of the woods."

Theo peered over the top of the tank. "Come help me, I think there's a copper shield against the wall." He pulled out a long curved object wrapped in plastic dry-cleaning bags. It was so tall it touched the ceiling as he pulled it from the tank.

"Oh dear, it's been bent." Laura looked at the shield and gasped. "Theo, it's 'Moon Man Eyes.' "

"Moon Man Eyes" was four feet of beaten copper divided one-fourth the way down by a raised ridge. Mounted in the upper section were two bronze Asian coins serving as irises for huge almond eyes that filled most of the upper field. The empty corners of the field were filled with geometric incisings of eyelids, brows, lashes, and extra helping eyes.

Reverently Theo said, "The coins must be ancient."

"Not that old, they were added much later. The important part of 'Moon Man Eyes' is the lower field. It's at least two hundred years old and no one's ever tampered with it."

"Is that writing on it?"

Laura nodded. "It's the Tsamian creation story. Except for petroglyphs, it's the only example of coastal pictographs in existence."

The bottom field was etched all over with tiny totemic figures. Some of the sketches were simple shorthand pictures of Northwest animals and features. Others were abstract shapes. The story started at the center top and read downward. At the bottom the figures split in two and swirled up both sides, like water in a closed space. The two parts eddied in and wound down into opposing spirals. Ravens and fishes were in the story, as were two snow-covered mountains.

"Can you read it?" he asked.

Laura straightened and responded with ceremonial words: "I can only read it as it was read to me."

"I see."

"Starting at center top: 'Raven left the snowland at the end of the world and came to the perfect place.' The perfect place is the three salmon."

"Abundance?"

"Yes. 'There were no people in the perfect place and most of the world was still water. The Dolphin People lived in the water and held evil away by singing both day and night: the men singing in the daytime and the women at night. Dawn and dusk were the only times they could meet.' "

"Poor devils."

" 'One day a Dolphin man with a new wife saw the Queen Charlotte Islands rising from the sea and said to Raven, "If you let me go there with my wife, I will do anything.'

"Starting up the other side: 'Raven said, "In the new place the work is very hard." Dolphin man replied, "I do not mind hard work, if only I can stop singing for the water-world." Putting Dolphin man and his wife in a clamshell, Raven washed them up on the beach. After a time Dolphin man was pleading with Raven to go back because the work was so hard, but in the end he stayed, because at night in the new place he could lie with his wife.' "

Theo raised his eyebrows. "Heavy-duty stuff."

"It never did much for me. I always wondered about the Dolphin woman."

"What do you mean?"

Laura shrugged. "I mean, why would she even go in the first place?"

Theo stared at her a moment and said, "I can tell you what my sister says about basketball."

"What's that?"

"Boys' rules make a better game."

Laura blinked. "How tall's your sister?"

"Same size as you. Name's Honorée."

"Honorée and Theophile. Anybody else?"

"No. How about you?"

"Two big brothers. My father's an orthodontist in Newport Beach." Theo took her gloved hand and squeezed it gently. "We need to talk here soon, lady."

Searching his eyes, she said, "Theo, I already told you: I live in Los Angeles."

"And that's your final word?"

"Yes."

"In that case we'd better inventory this stuff and get it back to town."

"Is everything out of the tank?" she asked.

"The rest looks like newspaper. That's too bad, I was hoping we'd find something to stick Siecetti to all this."

Peering into the tank, Laura spied a chunky brass zipper in the crumpled newsprint at the bottom. "The duffel! Help me get it out."

Theo moved a kitchen chair over and stood on it to reach the bottom of the tank. He bent over the side, his feet leaving the chair as he reached far down. Red-faced and puffing, he came up with the canvas duffel. "Empty," he said.

"Maybe." Laura stuck her hand in the bag and searched the corners. "Hurray!" She pulled out a packet of creamy envelopes and pocketed it in her warm-ups.

"I can't let you take those, they're evidence."

Laura glared. "Talbot, I can't believe you'd do this to me."

He waited without speaking as she took out the envelopes and handed them over. Putting them on the table next to the artifacts, he said, "There's nothing I can do about it right now. I promise to get them back to you when we're finished."

"That's not the problem," she said. "The problem is I helped Larry steal from the dig and wrote about it in the letters. Somebody will read them."

Theo looked away, then picked up the duffel. Paper crinkled inside. Pulling back the sides, he brought out several yellow carbon sheets. Scrutinizing them, he said, "These are from the post office. Todd shipped things to Italy: 'Number

Twelve Piazza Nessuno, Roma.' This is to somebody named V. Siecetti.''

"The dean! But his first name is Allesandro."

"And the dean doesn't live in Rome either. V. Siecetti must be a relative."

Laura's face lit up. "Now I see. They were shipping things to a relative in Rome."

"Sounds like it. How many Siecettis can there be in Rome?"

"There's a Roman phone book in the UCLA reference room. We could actually find out if we wanted."

"Laura the Literal."

Basking in the alliteration, she said, "Theo, whatever happens, you've been a lot of fun, okay?"

Outside they heard the wailing of a police siren far down the drive. Theo walked to the door and held it open for her. "Sorry, lady, you're not getting off that easily."

"But I stole from the dig, and smuggled things over the border. You'll lose your job if you hang around with me."

"Hey, lighten up." They watched as a revolving bank of car lights bathed the woods in red and blue. "When we finish at the station, I want to take you someplace I can cook a meal. All hanging around with you does is make me hungry."

CHAPTER 16

"Ho, are you up? You have company for breakfast." Laura stepped into his entry as the first rays of Sunday crossed the floorboards.

"Wait here, Theo, this is awfully early."

She walked down the paneled hall and knocked on the bedroom door. "Ho? Theo Talbot is here and he wants to make us a Creole breakfast. We've already been to the grocery store."

After a short silence Ho called through the door, "May I call Max?"

"Yes, do that. We bought four dozen oysters."

Back in the kitchen Theo brewed a pot of dark-roast coffee. He put Laura to the task of peeling oranges and slicing them in rounds. While the coffee was brewing he heated a pan of milk and when both were ready he poured the coffee and milk together half and half. Coffeemilk, he called it. As everyone sipped the fragrant brew, Theo expertly skewered long rows of bacon-wrapped oysters and made a hot sauce palatable for West Coast wimps.

"What's that?" Laura asked.

"A kind of piquante sauce."

"Pecan?"

"P-i-q-u-a-n-t-e. You sauté onions, add vinegar, tomato paste, Tabasco. It's for the oysters. Or eggs, it's nice on eggs."

"Why are we sprinkling powdered sugar on the oranges, aren't they sweet enough?"

"Set them in the sun and they'll make syrup. At home we use fresh figs."

Max arrived to the luscious scent of dark-roast coffee and broiling bacon. At first he kept Theo at arm's length, but after accepting coffeemilk and a skewer of oysters, the two men began talking cookery and crab pots and in a while were chatting away as Max basted the second batch of oysters.

Theo warmed croissants in a low oven and soon the apartment smelled like the French Quarter market. Laura offered to help carve honeydews for something called Melon Glissande and stood eagerly as Theo stirred creamed eggs in a double boiler. By the time he pronounced breakfast ready she was hungry enough to kill. She ate eggs, melon, orange compote, croissants and then went out to the living room to look for leftover oysters. Theo told the story of Siecetti to Ho and Max, who sat as fascinated as groundlings hearing of aristocratic disgrace. "He's our superior," explained Max.

"*Was*, Maximilian. Obviously he'll be replaced."

Max shook his head. "A very cerebral man, I wouldn't have thought it."

Theo broke in. "I can almost understand his motive in killing Larry and Adele Patterson when they crossed him, but the one I can't put together is why Siecetti'd get involved in something as dumb as stealing from museums."

Ho said, "I wish people hadn't whisked us out of here Friday in such a rush, I might have been able to prevent a great deal of grief if we had moved a bit slower then."

Laura said, "I don't think so, Ho. The man was armed and dangerous; it really was a police matter."

"That's not what I meant. Just a minute."

Ho left the room and returned with a dog-eared manila envelope from interlibrary loan. Handing it to Laura, he said, "This came Friday morning. I didn't have time to look at it before we left."

Laura slipped out an issue of *International Design*. It was oversized and glossy and $12.50 a copy. Ho said, "The article you're interested in is on page thirty-five."

Laura found the page and read the title, " 'Religious Primitives in the Modern Interior by Vittorio Siecetti.' "

Ho said, "I came across 'V. Siecetti' in *Reader's Guide* while looking for reviews on Dean Siecetti's new book. I started to wonder if our dean were related."

Scanning the article, Laura said, "I don't understand, this is about African art. God, will you look at this."

"What is it?"

She held up a full-page photo of a massive black mask mounted above a California abode fireplace. The mask was crowned with a pointed headdress and collared with a gold-and-ivory breastplate. The burnished face was melancholy and long, as if carved by a European mannerist. The heavy eyelids were half-closed over piercing eyes. The piece's long lines and fluted curves gave it a curiously elegant look—both intellectual and tragic. " 'Ashanti kingdom, the head of Christ,' " Laura read. "I've never seen anything like this before, the Ashanti are known for their magic masks."

Ho said, "Give me the article and I'll mark the salient paragraphs." He took a pen from his pocket and swiftly bracketed several paragraphs for her.

Taking back the magazine, Laura began reading: " 'Not only can religious primitives impart serious design suggestions, they can also—by previous cultural associations—lend understated authority and elegance to the modern interior. The austerity often ascribed to modern design can be substantially alleviated by bold integration . . .' Okay, skip down.

" 'As more European missions are being closed by the tide of third world nationalism, religious primitives are starting to find their way into the international marketplace. Serious collectors should consider the beauty and collectibility of these objects and be cognizant of their investment value.' "

"Keep reading."

" 'Although the illustrated articles are only a sampling from Africa, we must point out that the Dark Continent is not the only place from whence primitives emanate.

" 'In addition to the Portuguese flow of colonial African art we find that many Spanish reliquaries and museums are deaccessioning their New World collections. Not all the arriving Spanish pieces are the familiar pre-Columbian, however. Spanish expeditions ranged as far north as the Canadian coast of British Columbia and very occasionally these prized Northwest primitives will appear on the market. These pieces currently enjoy international vogue and are, at present, highly collectible.' "

Laura looked up indignantly. "That's a lie. Nobody has pieces that old. The rat's trying to drive up prices."

The phone rang and Ho pushed back his chair and stood up. "Now the best part," he said, "read 'About the Author.' " He went out to answer the phone and Laura read, " 'Doctor Vittorio Siecetti is a Roman art and antiquities dealer and consultant to the Vatican. His shop on the Piazza Nessuno has a full range of third world religious objects for the consideration of the serious collector. By appointment only.' " She turned to Theo. "It makes sense now. I can't believe it finally makes sense."

"May I see?"

Ho came back and said, "Laura, phone is for you."

Laura handed the magazine to Theo and got to her feet. Back in the study she carried the phone to the center of the rug to sit in a shaft of sunlight. "Hello."

"Laura, it's me."

"Bush, are you in town?"

"No, dummy, I'm in Seattle. Like you should be."

"Are we still in the tournament?"

"We're not only in, snookems, semi's are this afternoon. How about getting your fanny in gear?"

"You're mad."

"Laura, damn it, where've you been? A policeman sat in

the corridor all last night waiting for you. I didn't know whether we should hide you or turn you in."

"Everything's fine now."

"So you'll be here for the semi's?"

Theo walked in and leaned against the desk watching her.

"I can't make it, Bush. It's too late to get to Seattle in time; I couldn't get there if I wanted."

"Laura, we don't have six good players right now; Terri and K-Two are out with bad knees. Fly down, I'll pay for it."

"Can't. There aren't any flights out until afternoon on Sunday. And at your end it's another hour from the airport to the university. Sorry."

Theo raised his eyebrows and pointed to himself and the receiver. Laura handed it to him and lay down on the rug in the sun.

"Claudia? This is Theo Talbot, I talked to you yesterday. Well, the compliment is mutual. It sounds like you'll need her in a few hours." He listened for a moment, then said, "She's crazy, she's dying to play."

"Theo!" Laura grabbed for the receiver but he kept it out of reach.

"No, I can get her there for you . . . plenty of time . . ." He ducked and bobbed to keep the receiver from Laura. "Okay, see you there." And he hung up.

"Are you *nuts*? How are we going to get to Seattle?"

"Hey, lady, this is my best thing." And he thumbed the yellow pages until he found what he wanted. He pointed with his index finger to a place on a page.

"Dial this number, will you?"

Laura dialed and reached the recording for a seaplane charter service. "Ha, they don't fly on Sunday."

"Horse feathers, he flies whenever he can hustle the business. He's home working on his MG." Theo flipped through the white pages and took the phone from Laura.

"Angela, is Randy there? Good. Would you ask him if he could fly Theo Talbot and a friend from Bayside Park to Hec Edmondson pavilion in Seattle? Tell him the friend is an *important* sports figure." Laura shook her head and walked back to the kitchen for more coffeemilk.

Twenty minutes later, as she watched Randy taxi to the dock in his cream-and-green Beaver, Laura was feeling manipulated and used. The engine noise bored in their ears like a drill. To make her point she had to shout. "I'm going back to Los Angeles tonight!"

"I always knew you were," Theo shouted back.

"Although I'm very sad about it."

Theo didn't answer.

CHAPTER 17

Red-headed Randy wore shorts and flip-flops and a cast on his ankle. "Rugby," he explained succinctly, and he taxied across Bellingham Bay before they could change their minds about his ability to fly. Lifting the Beaver from the water, he leveled off at two thousand feet. He pointed out the white pyramid of Mount Rainier one hundred and fifty miles to the south, and soothed them with an old professional trick: "See? There's our landmark. Almost there."

They flew over islands with tiny cusp beaches and sailboats in secret harbors. On Puget Sound itself, freighters and ferries wore frothing white tails that stretched out miles behind. The Everett pulp mills reeked stench even at two thousand feet.

Theo sat up front with Randy reading from something in his lap. Engine noise made conversation impossible and Laura sat alone in back wondering if she was still loved. She looked down at the dreamy splendor, pretending that Theo Talbot didn't matter. As they approached Seattle and the university on Lake Washington, Randy stirred and looked at Theo for instructions.

"Circle the football stadium."

Randy banked to the right and they looked down on the campus. The first college buildings had been sited along a center axis pointing to Mount Rainier and from the air the campus looked like earth markings pointing to the great god Rainier.

Theo shouted, "See the dock by the crew house? She's playing volleyball next door in Edmondson Pavilion."

"We'll see what we can do." Randy flew to the south end of the lake, banked north, then slowly pushed in the wheel for a soft-angle landing next to the stadium. They settled gently on the water, then taxied to the crew dock, whorling cattails in their dirty air.

Randy nudged his pontoons up to the dock and reached over Theo to open the door. "Here we are, amigo." To Laura he said, "Win that tournament now."

"Piece of cake."

They watched Randy taxi out to the middle of the lake and with ear-piercing noise, peel the plane off the water, and raise it to the sky. He circled back over the dock and yawed back and forth waving good-bye. They laughed and waved back.

The sunny dock was suddenly quiet. Ducks appeared from the cattails and swam cautiously toward the new people on the dock. Laura looked at Theo, then picked up her garment bag.

"Wait," he said. "It'll be crowded inside and I want to talk to you alone."

"Please don't. I really have to go to L.A."

"That's not what I want to talk about." He reached in his breast pocket and pulled out a small packet. Her letters. "Have you read these?"

"I wrote them."

"But do you actually know what they say?"

"Mushy stuff to Larry; that I stole from the dig."

"Laura." He slipped a sheet of creamy paper out of an envelope and began reading: " 'Wasn't there another way to pay Jimmy B. for carving the fish clubs? We both know how the money was spent, we even know his favorite brand. Couldn't you at least have given the money to Mary Mac . . .' "

Laura put down her garment bag to listen.

"Or this one," he said. " 'Dear Larry, It was terribly wrong of me to bring the bracelets over without telling the Georges. I wish you had never asked because now I must deal with you on a level of mistrust I'm not very comfortable with . . .' "

"I remember that: 'A level of mistrust.' "

"I just skimmed these, but I don't see anything that's badly incriminating."

"But I helped him *steal*."

"And these letters make Larry Todd look guiltier than a snake. "And I can't see that they have any relevance to a homicide."

Laura contemplated the sky before speaking. "Max said you were a 'decent specimen.' "

"He did? That's pretty high praise coming from him."

"I think you're a decent specimen, too."

"I was hoping for a bit more than that."

"The only honest thing to say to you is that I have to go back to L.A."

"I know, and I have to go back to Bellingham."

"So what's left? 'It's been nice knowing you?' "

"Laura, I don't copulate on a nice-knowing-you basis and neither do you."

Laura reddened. "How do you know? You just met me."

Theo opened his mouth, then changed his mind. "I think I'll pass on that one." He put his hands in his pockets and looked at the water. "Is there someone in Los Angeles I don't know about?"

"The only person I care about in L.A. is my adviser."

"You really lead with your chin, don't you?"

"This is completely different; he's happily married and I like his wife. He's not Larry Todd."

"How about you, haven't you learned anything?"

"I learn all the time and I'll tell you a secret I learned from volleyball: You get good by hanging around the good people. You get in close enough to see how they work, breathe in their air. It's true in volleyball, and it's true in anthropology, at least with the ones who don't smoke.''

He crossed his arms.

''Theo, the people with the information are males, what am I supposed to do?''

''Have a little more self-respect.''

They heard a noise in the boathouse and turned to watch two fresh-faced crewmen emerge, carrying a racing shell over their heads. They watched as the students walked down the dock and flipped the shell neatly onto the water. The oarsmen climbed in, strapped on shoes, and rowed away.

When the boat was out of earshot and ducks were treading near the dock again Laura said, ''You know what you haven't told me? Friday night you said you knew something about us that I didn't.''

''Actually I know two things about us.''

''Okay, what's the first one?''

''The first one is I saw what you were trying to hide the morning we met in Larry Todd's office.''

''About my letters?''

''No. What you thought of me.''

''I didn't think anything about you, I'm good at hiding my feelings.''

''Laura, the way you looked at me was just about the most flattering thing that's ever happened.''

She took his hand and found he had two thickened knuckles from an old injury. Someday she would ask about them but not today. ''And what's the other thing you know about us?'' she asked.

''The other thing is that you feel just like Honorée to me.''

She dropped his hand. ''Ugh, that's sick.''

''On the contrary. I think it feels like it's supposed to.''

''You're serious, aren't you?''

''Try to guess.''

She narrowed her eyes. ''So what are we going to do?''

''I'm from the school of thought that believes if you aim in a certain direction, after a while you get there.''

''So what are you saying? I go back to L.A. and one day you magically show up on my doorstep?''

"Or, we both go home, run up huge phone bills and one day magically end up someplace else."

Laura picked up her garment bag and walked to the gym. Far be it from her to ruin his Disneyland.

He walked with her slowly down the gravel path, giving the waddling ducks time to fan out in front of them. Approaching the old brick pavilion they heard the echo of referee whistles. Theo stopped. "There's one more thing I should tell you."

"Theo, please don't."

"Laura, I love you very much."

Tears filled Laura's eyes. "I asked you not to."

"I said I love you."

"I know you did." She found a wadded Kleenex and wiped the corners of her eyes. "And now I have to say something to you." She blew her nose. "I didn't want to think about it until I was on the airplane home."

"Darling, if that's your worst problem, you're in great shape. Come here." He planted his feet and wrapped his arms around her.

Taking her chin in his hand he gently touched her mouth with his. She made no complaint and they kissed tranquilly, like lovers on a Sunday morning. When they finished Laura lifted her arms around his neck to feel his whole body and they kissed again, finding in it a way to temporarily ignore their knotty problem.

They pulled apart and walked the rest of the way to the gym. Theo opened the door to a waft of gymnasium smell. The acid scent enveloped them and they instantly became part of a volleyball crowd. Laura went to the balcony to look for the powder blue jerseys. Someone beside them said, "Laura, is that you?" They looked down to see Terri with her feet on a chair and Blue Ice on her knees.

"What did you do to your hair?" Terri asked.

"What did you do to your knees?"

"My knees are shit."

"Can't Norman do something?"

"Norman is shit. We broke up. I told him to take a flying leap."

Laura was speechless, so Terri spoke again, "Have you seen Bushman?"

"I haven't seen anyone, I just got here. Terri, this is Theo Talbot."

"Glad to meet you," said Terri. "Bushman told us about you. Laura, if you see Bushman ask her to coach. Unless you want to?"

"No, I'll find her, are you sure you're all right?"

"Hell no, I'm not all right. I broke off my engagement and my knees hurt like hell. If somebody could find me cortisone I'd eat the stuff."

"I'm sorry about Norman."

"Norman's a toad." They eyed each other, Terri shifting restlessly, looking for a posture with no pain. "Why did you cut your hair?"

"Like it?"

"Hell no."

"I'll tell you about it later. Who we playing?"

"UCLA. Tom Selleck's giving out the awards, so everyone's hot to beat them." Terri turned to Theo. "Did Laura tell you she likes Tom Selleck?"

"He's six-four," Laura explained.

There was a commotion in the stands and three neckless football linemen came in, scanning the balcony for bimbos and crazies. Tom Selleck entered, dazzlingly handsome in a white polo and chinos. His hair was thickly beautiful, as on television, and he oozed charisma the way others ooze aftershave.

"Theo, you can stay here if you like; Terri and I have to go down on the floor."

"I'll say we do," said Terri. "Here comes Norman." She stood up stiffly and leaned on Laura's shoulder. Norman approached but before he could speak Terri turned and snapped, "Norman, I don't want to hear about it." Laura helped her down to the floor and then to arrange her legs on a folding chair.

"You'd better go warm up," said Terri.

"If I warmed up, I'd fall over. I don't think I care about volleyball right now."

"Sure you do, big *D* for desire."

"Big *D* for degenerating."

"What happened, Laura? About your hair and everything?"

"It's pretty complicated, it might be in the papers."

"Bushman's really upset, she says you ran off and left her at the shopping mall. She considers you her best friend, you know."

"I can't be the kind of friend Bushman needs right now," said Laura.

"She's not going to bother you, she knows you like guys."

Laura picked at her shoelaces. "I know that. It's just that she's got to stop pretending we're all twenty year olds living happily ever after in a gymnasium."

They looked at the laughing black Westwood teenagers on the far court and the young Floridians warming up on their side.

"We don't have a good attitude," said Laura.

"We don't have a good team."

They eyed each other soberly. Laura finally said, "Rookie's going to be disappointed."

Terri shifted in the chair. "She needs to lose a little, keep her humble." Calling to the Gatoraders, she said, "Where's Bushman?"

"I saw her in the locker room."

Bushman came out carrying her shoes and some Blue Ice and sat down silently beside Laura. She slapped it on her knees and bent stiffly to tie her shoes. The announcer came on the PA for their game and began calling out the Westwood lineup. Laura recognized no names, hearing only the impressive heights: "six-three," he said, "six-five, six-two." She sat stonily, understanding only that volleyball had somehow passed her by while she wasn't looking.

Turning to Bushman, she asked, "How you going to play with your knees like that?"

"Just play. My father called again for you, he's driving me crazy. Either you, or I, are supposed to call him back."

"What does he want?"

"He wants to know if you can teach Larry Todd's summer

classes. He said to tell you, 'Intro and Cultural and the text-books are ordered.' We're supposed to call him back today.''

Laura looked up at Theo in the stands. He smiled back and lifted a hand in greeting. "Today?" she asked. "Tell him I'd love to try.''

ABOUT THE AUTHOR

Linda Mariz, who holds degrees in American history, is currently a triathlete and masters swimmer. She lives with her husband and two children in coastal Washington state.